NOT A WEREWOLF

NOT A WEREWOLF

JAKE & BOO - BOOK 1

Madeline Kirby

Not a Werewolf by Madeline Kirby

Cover Design: Madeline Kirby

Madeline.Kirby.Author@gmail.com
www.evilgeniusatwork.com

ISBN: 978-1517314569

Dedication

For my Breakfast Club – the Divas,
the Goddesses, my road trip buddies.
And of course my husband, the Honorary Goddess
and all-around good sport.

Behave yourselves, and don't eat too much jerky.

Table of Contents

Jake Is Not a Werewolf

"I THINK I might be a werewolf."

"I think you've been reading too many paranormal romance novels."

"Well, something's wrong with me, and that's the only explanation I can think of that makes any sense."

"Dude, it makes *no* sense. There's no such thing as werewolves."

I tried growling at my best friend, but he just gave me a funny look, with his upper lip kind of pulled up on one side, letting me know what he thought of that. I had to admit it didn't sound very convincing. Maybe I wasn't cut out to be a werewolf. I tried growling again, to make sure.

"You're not a werewolf, Jake. Shut up."

"Maybe I'm one of those submissive werewolves. An Omega or whatever." I was still hung up on the growling thing.

"Not. A. Werewolf." Don repeated, not lifting his eyes from the book he was reading. He turned the page, as if I hadn't just dropped a paranormal bomb on him. His best friend might be a werewolf, and he was fucking reading a book?

"What are you reading?" I asked, to make conversation and get his attention back on me.

"*World War Z*."

"Isn't that about zombies?" I asked.

"Yep."

"So you don't believe in werewolves, but you believe in zombies?"

Don closed the book and rubbed at a spot between his eyes. "No. I do not believe in zombies. I am entertained by zombies."

"I don't think I like your tone."

"You don't like my tone? Really? You know, you could not like my tone from your own apartment."

"What the fuck? Fine." I opened the door onto the hall, leaving it standing open as I left because I knew that irritated him and he'd have to get up to close it. I marched across the landing and opened the door to my own apartment before turning back to deliver my parting shot. "Just be careful on the next full moon, dude. I'll be watching for you."

Don's witty comeback was an elegantly extended middle finger. He'd gotten really good at that gesture since we'd met. I flopped down on my sofa and looked out the window while I waited for Don to come over and continue the conversation.

My squirrel was back. Well, not mine, obviously, but the one who hangs out in the live oak outside my apartment and watches me through the windows, the furry little perv. He was nibbling on an acorn, spinning it around in his sharp little claws while he watched me like I was an exhibit at the zoo. Maybe to squirrels, that's what humans inside their houses are. Maybe we're just entertainment for them.

"Okay, fine. Why do you think you're a werewolf?" I turned to see Don leaning against the doorframe, arms crossed.

I didn't say anything, just frowned and turned back to watch my voyeuristic squirrel.

"Dude, come on. You look like hell, you've been acting loopy all week, and now this werewolf stuff. What's going on?"

I sighed and swung my legs to the floor so Don could join me on the sofa. "I haven't had a decent night's sleep in days. I have these crazy dreams that seem to go on and on, and I wake up exhausted."

"And that translates to you being a werewolf how?"

"The dreams are the same every night – well, pretty much. I'm running and smelling things and hunting. I'm running on four legs and I have fur and paws, I can see them when I look down. I don't really think clearly in my dreams – I mostly *feel* stuff."

"Like what?"

"Happy, frightened, excited. Nothing complicated. But I run and run, and it's so vivid. Like I'm really there, and I wake up feeling like I was."

"Maybe you're just not sleeping well. Have you tried taking a sleep aid?"

"Yeah, but that just made it worse. Like I was still there, but having trouble keeping up – like walking against the tide."

"Okay, I get that you're having some kind of sleep issues and crazy dreams, but the werewolf thing is over the top. Maybe you're sleepwalking?"

That sounded better than being a werewolf, even though werewolves were pretty cool. "But, wouldn't that be dangerous? Like, what if I'm sleepwalking and get hit by a car crossing the street, or head over to the park and fall into the bayou or something?"

Don rested his head on the back of the sofa and looked at the ceiling. "I haven't heard you leave your apartment, though, and I think I would."

Yeah, that was pretty likely. It was an old building, one of those early twentieth century rooming-style buildings with eight studio apartments, each with a bathroom and a tiny kitchen. There was a wide hallway that ran through the center of the building from front to back on both floors. The original wooden interior doors were still there, and there were gaps between the bottoms of the doors and the floor.

"Yeah. Whatever."

"Jake…"

"Yeah, yeah. I know. Maybe it's nerves. Midterms are coming up in a couple of weeks."

"Pfft. Since when have you worried about school?"

"Since my advisor told me I needed to stop putzing around and settle on a major. He seems to think seven years is long enough to make up my mind."

"He may have a point."

I shrugged.

"You want to talk about it?"

"I just… I just really like studying, you know? There's so much, and I want to learn so much of it. How can I possibly make up my mind? How can I pick just one thing?"

"Just because you graduate doesn't mean you have to stop going to school. Or you could double major. That squirrel is starting to freak me out."

The squirrel had moved to sit on the windowsill and was watching us through the slightly rippled glass.

"He's probably just hungry."

"You've been feeding it, haven't you?"

"Sometimes I put some sunflower seeds on the windowsill. The occasional pecan. Maybe."

"What if it has rabies?"

"He doesn't have rabies."

"How do you know? Are you an animal expert now? Maybe you should transfer to A&M."

"Yeah, and my fine gay ass would last how long in College Station? No, thank you very little, I'll stay right here." I looked at the squirrel, who had started scratching at the window. "I just know. I don't know how I know, but I know."

"You definitely need a good night's sleep. You're getting loopier by the minute."

I didn't answer. I got up to fetch a handful of sunflower seeds from the kitchen and crossed back over to the window.

"Whoa. Are you going to open that window?"

"Duh."

"What if it tries to come inside?"

"He won't. And if he does I'll put him back out. Just chill."

The squirrel was looking at Don now, and when I raised the window he started making that annoyed chirpy noise they make when someone is in their territory. I don't think he liked Don any more than Don liked him. "Now, now. Hush, you." I sprinkled the seeds on the windowsill and the squirrel decided they were more interesting than Don and dug into his snack. I closed the window and left him to it. "Miss Nancy says –"

"Oh, lord. Miss Nancy? Now we're getting somewhere." Don did not think much of my spiritual advisor.

"Miss Nancy has a gift." She did, too. I had known Miss Nancy since I was twelve, and she had guided me over many a bump in my adolescent road. She always encouraged me to trust myself and never flipped me off or called me loopy. "And I'm going to see her tomorrow."

"You're going to do what you want to do, no matter what I say."

"Yeah."

"Okay, fine. I gotta go – I'm working happy hour today. You want to come by? I can hook you up with a beer or two."

"Probably not. Maybe I'll try to go to bed early."

Jake Finds Something on a Bridge

I DIDN'T sleep any better that night than I had the rest of the week. I woke up grumpy and too unfocused to bother with making my own coffee, so I walked a few blocks to the local coffee shop, Ground Up. Harry was working the counter and fixed me a large French press all for myself without batting an eye. I must have looked like death warmed over.

I found a table in a corner and was waiting for my coffee to finish doing its thing when the chair across from me slid out and a cappuccino and scone were plopped down on the table.

"Figured you'd be here. You get any sleep last night?" Don asked.

"Not much."

"Dreams again?"

I nodded.

"So, do you remember these dreams in detail?"

I pushed the plunger on the coffee pot and tried to remember something concrete from last night's dreams.

"There was a lot going on. I remember at one point I was walking along the bayou, and I wanted to get closer. There was something that I wanted to smell, or something like that. I just remember the feeling of wanting something. But then something distracted me, or pulled me away, or something – I don't know."

"Is that it?"

"Later – I don't know how much later – I remember feeling afraid." I paused to take a sip of coffee. "There were these, I don't know, shadows or shapes, and they were making a lot of noise."

"What kind of noise?"

I closed my eyes and tried to concentrate. "It was like… yelling. Like when kids are playing and getting rowdy and talking trash. That kind of thing. But there were a bunch of them, a group, and I was afraid, so I ran and hid."

"That doesn't sound like a very werewolf-like reaction."

I gave Don the best glare I could manage in my exhausted state. "So you're an expert now? I'm new at this, okay? And maybe… maybe I'm some other kind of shifter?"

"Oh geez, what have you been reading now? Other kind of shifter?"

"Can we get back to my dream, please?"

"Fine. So what happened next?"

"The shadows – I guess maybe they *were* rowdy teenagers – moved on, and I came out of my hiding place. I think I was underneath some bushes. Anyway, I came out and started walking along the bayou again. I had walked a ways when I heard crying."

"Like a baby?"

"No. Some kind of animal. A kitten, I think. I followed the sound to where that old railroad trestle crosses the bayou. Where the bike trail is."

"And?"

"I could hear it – it sounded really scared and sad – but I couldn't find it. I kept looking, and I started getting worked up and anxious and that's when I woke up."

Don downed the last of his drink and wrapped what was left of his scone in a napkin. "Okay, let's go."

"What? Where?"

"To the trestle – the bike trail. Come on."

"But my coffee! I *need* this."

Don went up to the counter and Harry gave him a big to-go cup for the rest of my coffee. I let Don drag me out of the shop and down the street. "What are we doing?"

"We are going to go to the trestle and see if we find a lost kitten or whatever. Maybe if we go to the scene of the dream it will help somehow."

I wasn't so sure, but I figured it couldn't hurt. We were only a few blocks from where the trail crossed the bayou, so what did I have to lose but a little time?

We were the only ones on the trestle – the early morning cyclists and joggers were gone by now and people with normal jobs were at work. There was some highway noise, but we were used to that.

"Okay, here we are," Don said. "Do you remember where you were in your dream?"

I looked around, trying to remember shapes and angles from the dream. It had been dark, but I had been able to see pretty well. "I remember that," I said, pointing to the distinctive shape of a Quonset hut to our north. "I remember going up there because I smelled wood and I wanted to look for rats."

"Ew."

I ignored him and turned to look over the railing. "So I was on the north bank, under the trestle."

We stood there for a minute looking around, listening to the traffic whiz by on the highway.

"Hear any kittens?" Don asked.

"Ha ha. I'm not sure what we're supposed to be doing here."

"I don't know. I just figured, it was close so what was the harm in checking it out, if it would help."

"Yeah. It makes sense. You hear anything?"

"Nope."

We stood there for another minute, not hearing anything but the sound of traffic and some banging sounds from the nearby lumberyard. A long-legged bird was high-stepping around in the water below, looking for something to eat.

Don sighed. "Maybe –"

And then we heard it. In one of those rare soundless moments in the middle of all that noise we heard the saddest, tiniest mewing sound I'd ever heard. All the cute cat videos on the internet had not prepared me for that sound.

"Ohmigod! Ohmigod ohmigod. Did you hear that?" I started spinning around, trying to figure out where the sound had come from.

"Okay, calm down. It's obviously not here on the bridge. You stay here." Don jogged back to end of the bridge and took a dirt path down the slope. When he got to the bottom he looked up to where I was standing on the bridge.

"Do you see anything?" I called down.

"Not yet." Don was looking around on the ground, up the slope, and then up to where I stood on the bridge. "Maybe. About six feet to your right. A little farther. There. There's something hanging from the bridge."

I looked down and could see a piece of twine tied around one of the upright posts of the bridge railing. "There's something tied to the railing."

"Can you pull it up?"

"Ohmigod. What if it's – I don't know – gross or creepy or something?"

"Dude, it was alive a few seconds ago, right? If that's it we've gotta help it."

"Right." He was right, so I managed to get my hand down between the rails and started pulling up whatever was hanging from the twine. It wasn't heavy, and it didn't seem to be moving. When I got it up far enough I could see it was a cheap drawstring bag. It wouldn't fit between the horizontal railings, so I had to work it up, one rail at a time. By the time I got it high enough to reach from above, Don had made it back up to the bridge and lifted it over. He put it on the pavement between us and started working on the knot that was holding the bag closed.

I could see the bag move a little, and then I heard that sad little mewing again. "Hurry!"

"I'm trying!"

"The office at the lumberyard should be open by now. Let's go over there and ask if we can borrow some scissors and cut it open."

"Yeah." Don scooped up the bag. "No, it's still tied to the bridge. Shit!"

I leaned over to where the twine was fastened to the upright. Maybe a different person had tied this knot, or whatever sick asshole had done this wasn't as concerned about the bag staying tied to the bridge as he was about keeping the bag closed, and that knot came apart quickly.

We jogged to the lumberyard office, Don cradling the bag and me clutching my half-finished coffee.

The guy in the office must have been shocked when we stumbled in, panting and rambling, but he figured out what we needed and pulled some big scissors out of the desk. Don put the bag down on a table, and the lumberyard guy and I stood on either side of him while he carefully cut the bag open.

I was holding my breath as Don looked inside the bag, then reached in and pulled out a tiny kitten. It wiggled a little and mewed again, and I was able to start breathing again. "Is it okay?"

Don looked it over. "I'm no expert, but it's probably hungry and scared. We need to take it to a vet. Oh, poor thing – it only has three legs."

"What? What did those monsters do?!"

"Chill, Jake. It looks like he was born this way. That's probably why those creeps decided to pick on it."

"Gosh," said the lumberyard guy – I looked, but he wasn't wearing a nametag or one of those shirts with his name on it. "You found this little guy? In that bag?"

"Yeah," Don said, cradling the kitten against his chest. "We think some kids put it in that bag and then tied it to the bridge."

"Damn. That's sick."

"Yeah!" I said. "Someone should –"

"Jake," Don cut me off. "Let's get going. I want to get him to a vet."

"Oh. Sure."

We thanked the lumberyard guy – whose name turned out to be Jake, too – and went back out to the bike trail.

"Should we walk back home and get your car?" Don asked. "Or walk?"

"Walk?"

"Yeah – if we take the trail it takes us to the shopping center where there's one of those big pet stores with a clinic."

"Let's just walk. I don't need to go to class today."

"What about your appointment with Miss Nancy?"

"I'll cancel. It's cool. I can see her tomorrow."

We walked, and it was nice, actually. Early March in Houston was a good time to be outside and the sunshine was cheering me up. Don was still cradling the kitten, stroking it and murmuring to it, and I had a feeling he was going to keep it.

❧

While Don took the kitten to the back of the store to see the vet, I grabbed a cart and flagged down one of the workers to find out what I needed to get to set up housekeeping for a kitten. I piled a bunch of stuff in the cart – a litter box, some litter, a scooper. I looked at the dishes, but there were too many to decide between, so I decided Don could use his own dishes and get fancy cat dishes on his own later. The toys were cute, though, so I bought some catnip mice, and a feathery thing, and something on a string that it could chase. I wasn't sure how well it would be able to run on three legs, but Don could worry about that. I got a cardboard scratcher thing, too. Don's furniture was pretty shabby, but it didn't deserve to get ripped to shreds. I knew enough about cats to know they had a reputation in that area.

I took a turn down the food aisle, but decided I'd better wait and see what the vet said. I pushed the cart back to the clinic area, but Don was nowhere to be seen.

"Are you looking for the man with the kitten?" the girl behind the desk asked.

"Yeah. Is he in with the vet?"

"Yes. He's been in there for a while, so it shouldn't be too much longer."

I sat on a bench to wait for Don and pulled out my phone. I wished I had brought something to study – midterms really were coming up soon. I checked my email, but nothing new there. I had just started a Sudoku puzzle when Don came out, still cradling the kitten. He was totally keeping it.

"So, what did the vet say?" I asked as Don sat down next to me.

"Dehydrated, hungry, but mostly okay. He wasn't out there long enough to cause any lasting harm. We found him pretty quick…"

We both sat there for a minute, not saying anything. I was thinking about how we had found him. Why we had found him.

"Dude…"

"Yeah." I said. Don must have been thinking similar thoughts.

"Dude, you knew he was there. That's…"

"Something we can talk about when we get home, okay?"

"Okay." Don turned his attention back to the kitten. I had to admit it was pretty cute. It – he – had brown and black stripes and a white chin. The skin around his big round eyes was black, which made him look like he was wearing eyeliner. A little goth kitty – so cute. Don started rubbing his belly with a couple of fingers and he closed his eyes and started purring. Even if Don hadn't already decided, I had. He was keeping the kitten. Don needed the kitten.

"What are you going to name him, then?"

"Huh?"

"Your kitten. What are you naming him?"

"Oh, I can't keep – Jake, what is all that stuff?"

"Cat stuff. You are so keeping the kitten."

"Jake, I can't afford a pet. I'm trying to save up to go back to school."

"Then we'll share the kitten. I'll buy this stuff, and we'll figure out the rest as we go along, but he has to stay at your place. I don't think my squirrel would like him."

Don turned back to the kitten, but I knew it was partly to hide behind his long, dark bangs. "Okay." That was easy. I knew he wanted to keep it.

"Great. So what are you naming him, and what kind of food do we need to get?"

❧

It was a testament to the power of our friendship that I helped him schlep all that stuff home. It was only about a mile, but it was heavy, and I carried most of it because he was carrying Bridger. Yeah, we were walking back across the bridge where we found him when Don got that brilliant idea. Whatever – it was his cat. I guess if it had been a girl cat he would have named her Bridget.

Don was rattling on about follow-up appointments and getting Bridger neutered and making sure he stayed inside and yakity yakity I lost track by the time we got home.

Bridger pussy-footed around Don's apartment, sticking his little nose into every corner, while we set up his litter box and Don put some food and water down for him. We showed him where everything was, and then hoped for the best. He seemed to be settling in okay, and Don was totally captivated, so I headed back to my own place to get some studying done.

I curled up on the sofa to review some of my notes, but I couldn't concentrate. I started thinking about my dream, and about how I had heard the kitten in my dream, and then we found him. Either I *was* a werewolf (or whatever), or I had been sleepwalking and seen something, or this was the craziest coincidence ever, or… I didn't know what. I put my head back, closed my eyes, and for the first time in days I managed to get some sleep.

Jake Discovers Something Unpleasant

DON WAS too busy having a love fest with Bridger to worry about heavy discussions. And then he woke me from the first decent sleep I'd had in days to go kitten-sit the little terror while he went to work, so I didn't really talk to him again until the next morning.

I had to admit he was cute. Bridger, not Don. He was fluffy, and his eyes were still kind of blue – I remember Don saying something earlier about them not being their permanent color yet. He hopped around the room okay, bouncing a little like a rabbit with that one back leg. I could tell he wanted up on the sofa with me but hadn't figured out how to do that yet, so I took pity on him and scooped him up.

"Okay, pest. But if you need to pee you have to get down. Do not pee on me. Got it?"

He looked up at me, tilted his head, flopped onto my belly and started to purr. I took that as a yes and cracked open my books.

I must have fallen asleep and Don just left me there, because I woke up early the next morning on Don's sofa, covered with a blanket, and Don and Bridger were sacked out on Don's futon mattress. It was nice of him to let me sleep – lord knows I needed it – but my neck hurt and I had a sour taste in my mouth. But it was what woke me up that had me rushing to toss my cookies in Don's toilet.

Bridger came trotting into the bathroom and watched me from a safe distance.

"It's okay, kitty," I told him, wiping my chin with a piece of toilet paper and turning to rinse my mouth in the sink. "It's not, but it's okay."

"Jake?" Don was in the doorway, rubbing his eyes. He was wearing a ratty pair of plaid sleep pants and an old white t-shirt with a frayed hem. "You okay?"

"Dream." I rinsed my mouth again and washed my hands.

"A dream, like about Bridger?"

"Yeah."

"What was it? Should we… Is it something we should check out?"

"So you believe me now?"

"Not that you're a werewolf." Don turned and headed for his tiny kitchen. I really hoped he was making coffee. "But your dreams… I can't believe I'm saying this… but your dreams mean something. When I think of Bridger, hanging there, and maybe no one would ever have found him if you hadn't had that dream."

He put a plate of food down for the fuzzball and finally turned his attention to making coffee.

"It was pretty awful this time." I said after a minute.

"Like, how bad? Too bad to talk about?"

"No." I leaned against the doorframe and watched the coffee drip into the pot. "But give me a minute to process. It's barely six o'clock."

I went back into the bathroom to take care of some personal business then let Don have his turn. I helped myself to a cup of coffee and sat on the sofa to wait. When Don came back he had dressed and had a mug of his own. "Okay. Lay it on me."

"It was like the night before. I was walking along the bayou, on one of the trails. I was having a great time, smelling things and stopping to piss on things."

"Ew."

"Shut up. Anyway, I was really happy, and that was because I wasn't alone."

"Who – or what – was with you?"

"I don't know. I didn't get a good look. But I could tell it was someone I… that I *adored.* Like the sun rose and set on whoever – or whatever – I was with. And then there was this… this noise that startled me."

"What kind of noise?"

"I don't know. A squeaking sound. And whoever I was with got upset, I could sense it, and that made me upset. And then someone else was there – a person – yes, it was people. Two people. And they were arguing and I was getting upset. And then I smelled – well, I didn't, but in my dream I did – I smelled what in my dream I knew was fear. And then I smelled blood and I started to run, but I got caught on something. Whoever I was with – it was their blood – and I've never felt so *sad* and, and *helpless.* It was horrible."

"Wh – what happened then?"

"I kept trying to get away – I was afraid that I would get hurt, too. I kept pulling, and something finally gave way and I ran for cover. I don't remember much after that. I kept waking up and going back to sleep, but every time I'd really get to sleep I'd wake up again because I was so scared."

"It sounds like… gosh…"

"Yeah. I know what it sounds like."

"Hell's bells, Jake. What if we go down to the bayou and there's been, like… like…"

"Yeah."

"I think we need to go, though. Don't you?"

I looked down at my coffee. "Yeah. You're right. Give me a few minutes."

I gathered my books and went across the hall to my apartment where I set a new land speed record for showering and brushing my teeth. The dream and its aftermath had left me feeling dirty and gross.

I met Don on the landing. "Not bringing Bridger with us?" I asked.

"He's young and impressionable. He doesn't need to see this kind of thing."

"Geez, dude. Whatever, come on."

It was barely six-thirty, and the sun wasn't quite up yet. We were only a few blocks from Stude Park, and the bayou trails, so we were there in a few minutes. We took the trail between the ball fields and down towards the water.

"So," Don said, as we stood on the trail near the top of the concrete slope leading down to the brown water below us. "Which way?"

I looked back and forth, then pointed to our left. "That way. Near the trees."

We followed the trail as it hugged the top of the slope. This stretch always made me nervous – I could see myself slipping and rolling down the bank to the dirty water below. I relaxed as the trail veered left, away from the water and towards the trees. As we approached the footbridge that spanned one of the little gullies that led into the bayou I slowed, looking around.

"What?" Don asked.

"I think it was around here."

"Okay. Let's stay on the trail, in case, I don't know, there's evidence or something in the grass."

"Yeah."

We walked on until we were standing on the bridge, and I knew I needed to look down, but I just couldn't bring myself to do it.

"Dude…"

"What? What is it?"

I heard the sound of Don dialing on his phone. Only three digits, so I knew what that must be. I looked down, and there he was, in the gully and almost into the bayou itself. He was face down, so I don't know what he looked like, but he was wearing what looked to be a pretty expensive overcoat and loafers. He didn't have much hair, and what he had was grey, so he wasn't young. His arms were spread wide, and in his right hand he held a plastic bag. His left hand looked red and rough, like it had been hurt. Maybe he tried to defend himself. Or maybe it got banged up when he went down the embankment. Whoever did it must have pushed him over.

"You okay?" Don was asking. He must have finished his phone call.

I shook my head.

"You gonna throw up again?"

I shook my head again.

"The police are on their way."

"Okay." My voice sounded broken and weak. I did not want this to be real. At first I thought it might be kind of cool, but now Don had a cat, a man was dead, and I didn't know what I was anymore.

"Dude. Jake. Listen to me. We were out for a walk, okay? You can't tell the police that you dreamed this. Got it?"

I nodded. "We went for a walk." I looked across the bayou to the far bank and the highway, and the skyline beyond. Behind us the ground sloped up towards White Oak Drive. I turned to look. The trees would block the view from the houses there, and it would have been dark at night. Anyone looking out from up there would probably be looking at the skyline, anyway.

I could hear sirens in the distance, and Don's voice seemed to be coming from far away, reminding me not to tell the police I had dreamed about this. I nodded, but I was trying to concentrate on what I remembered from the dream, and how it fit in with what I was seeing.

"The dog," I said.

"What?" The sirens were closer, and I could see red and blue flashing lights in the distance.

"Where did the dog go?" I knew now that that's what I had sensed - the consciousness of a dog, this man's dog, terrified and gutted by the death of its master and fleeing in fear of the attacker. What was I missing? I - it - wouldn't have gone far.

"What are you talking about?"

"The bushes." I walked back to the west end of the bridge and looked around. The sirens had stopped, and I could see red and blue flashing lights through the trees. Voices carried down to where I was - I had left the trail and crossed to the small stand of trees, crouching down to peer into the bushes there.

I could hear Don calling to me, telling me to come back to the bridge. I could hear other voices, some of them were probably shouting at me, but I couldn't stop. That's when I spotted him, pressed back against a tree, as far up under a bush as he could get - a fluffy white West Highland terrier, looking a little worse for wear after spending a night in the dirt. He whined when he saw me, but he didn't growl, so I held my hand out for him to sniff. I talked nonsense to him, and he started inching forward. I could see he was wearing a collar, and a leash was still attached to it.

When he got close enough, I reached forward and hooked my fingers through his collar so he couldn't make a break for it. I got my other hand underneath him, and finally stepped back, lifting him up and holding him against my chest. I turned around to a scene out of a TV show. Police officers were putting up yellow tape and there were crime scene people searching the ground. Don was talking to one of the police officers, and an angry woman in a suit was bearing down on me.

"Who are you, and what are you doing over there?" She had a head full of tiny corkscrew curls, and I'd bet she was pretty when she wasn't scowling. She was just a little shorter than me, and I looked down to see that she was wearing Dr. Martens boots, not high heels like the lady detectives on TV. I guessed that made sense, but it brought home again that this was real life, and had to be dealt with.

"Uh – Jake Hillebrand. I was getting this dog… from under the bushes.'

"Is that your dog?" Her light brown eyes narrowed.

"No, ma'am." I shook my head.

She reached out a hand - I guess to look at the dog's tag - and he growled, pressing back against me. I held him close and bounced him a little, which seemed to calm him. She pulled her hand back and scowled some more.

"Can you read his tag?"

I fumbled with his collar, and turned the little bone-shaped tag so I could see the engraving. "Murphy, and there's a phone number."

"What is it?" she asked, pulling out a notepad and writing it down as I read the number out loud. "Don't go anywhere, Jake Hillebrand. And don't let that dog out of your sight. Go stand over there – with that guy," she pointed to Don and I nodded.

"Yes, ma'am."

I made my way over to where Don was standing on the bridge.

"I told you to stay on the trail," Don scolded me.

"He was scared and hiding. I couldn't just leave him there."

A buzzing came from below us and one of the crime scene people called out, "the victim's phone is ringing!"

"What's the number?" the curly-haired detective called from the top of the slope.

"713-555-8389."

"That's me. Let it ring." The ringing stopped and she cursed before taking her phone from her ear and disconnecting. "You find a wallet or ID on him?"

"Not yet."

"What's in that bag he's holding?"

"Dog poop."

She sighed and turned to where we stood. "Stay there!"

We nodded. After that it was lots of waiting while cops and forensic people swarmed all over the place. A police officer took down our information and we told him that we found the victim, Don called the police, we didn't know who the victim was, and we hadn't seen anything. Detective Perez - I had heard someone call her that - came over and glared at me some more and tried to take Murphy from me. The dog growled again and she backed off.

"Dude," Don said in a low voice so only I could hear. "I think that's Clarence Wilton."

"Huh?"

"The dead guy. I think it's Clarence Wilton, the developer."

"That asshole who's buying up bungalows and building those giant monstrosities? Half the neighborhood probably wants him dead. Maybe someone figured they were performing a public service."

"Shh. But yeah, I think it's him."

"Damn."

Murphy had stopped shaking, and I was getting tired of holding him, so I sat him on the ground and slipped my hand through the loop on the end of his leash. I remembered how Wilton's left hand looked roughed up, and realized it must have happened when Murphy made a break for it. I pulled my hand out of the loop and picked the dog up again. They'd probably want to check the leash for something.

A while later a woman in a forensic team jacket came over to check out the dog. She took his leash and put it in an evidence bag. I held Murphy while she wiped at his paws and checked him over. He didn't growl at her like he had at the detective, but he still didn't want to leave me.

"He seems to have formed an attachment to you," she said.

"I fished him out from the bushes over there," I told her, nodding to where I had found Murphy. "I think he was just scared and latched on. And animals seem to like me."

"We've got a family member coming who can take him, but if you can stay until then, it would be a big help. We don't have anyone to spare to watch the dog."

I nodded, and she went back to whatever it was she did.

A few minutes later a woman and a young man arrived. She was in her fifties, I figured. Well groomed, well dressed, composed and classy. The young man with her looked a little familiar. He was younger than me, I guessed. Maybe I'd seen him around campus. They both looked upset, and were talking to Detective Perez. Talking to Detective Perez sure upset me, so I sympathized with them. Perez pointed towards us, and they turned to look. The young guy started to move towards us, but Perez said something to him and he turned back. After a minute he nodded, then walked over to where we stood.

"I'm not supposed to talk to you," he said. "But thanks for taking care of Murphy. I can take him now." He held out his arms, and Murphy finally started showing a little enthusiasm, his tail wagging and his front paws stretching towards the young man.

"He's had a fright," I said, handing Murphy over.

The young man nodded, taking Murphy and walking back to where Detective Perez was waiting with the older woman, who we figured must be his mother and Wilton's wife – widow, now. As they approached the women, Murphy started straining and yapping. He must really not like Detective Perez. I heard the young man say he'd take Murphy to the car, and Perez nodded, frowning.

Without Murphy to watch, I started paying more attention to what was going on around me. There were people milling around, putting things in bags and taking pictures. Someone was looking at the body, but I didn't want to look down there, so I looked up, towards the road, and farther away to either side. Beyond the tape, onlookers had started to gather. Joggers and cyclists, mommies and nannies with strollers, a couple of reporters with cameras, people from the nearby houses who would have been attracted by the noise and flashing lights. The online neighborhood message board was probably already full of posts and idle speculation.

There was a man standing a little apart from the crowd, not talking and gossiping like the others. He was about halfway up the hill towards the road, holding a leash with a bulldog at the other end. He looked grim, but not shocked or horrified like the rest of the gawkers. He just stood there, frowning and watching. After a couple of minutes, a woman went up to him and said something. He didn't say anything, just shook his head, then turned and walked away, towards the houses. She watched him for a few seconds, then turned and walked towards one of the groups of people gathered along the perimeter formed by the yellow police tape.

Don elbowed me in the ribs. "Ow! Don't do that!" Don had really bony elbows.

"She's coming back. The lady detective."

"Perez."

"Yeah. She's got someone with her this time."

I sighed and turned back to watch Detective Perez and the new guy walk towards us. When they were a few feet away, they stopped, exchanged a few more words, and she stalked off. The new guy turned to face us, and I have to admit I lost all my focus.

He was big, well-dressed, and already had a heavy five o'clock shadow and it wasn't even lunch. He looked totally fierce. Like, violent fierce, not fabulous fierce. Although, I had to admit he looked pretty fabulous, too, with dark wavy hair and the brightest green eyes I had ever seen. .

"Are you a werewolf?" I asked, because something about this guy obliterated any filter I might have. Yeah, I was back on that, because this guy had to, *had* to be a total alpha male if I'd ever seen one. I wanted to roll over and show him my belly. I'd heard werewolves were hot, but wow.

"Huh?" He looked me up and down like he'd never seen anything like me before. Maybe he hadn't.

"Uh… nothing."

"Is your friend okay?" the werewolf asked, looking over my head at Don.

"Not really," Don said. "I think he might be having a psychotic break."

"I am *not* having a psychotic break. Don't be an asshole in front of Mister…?"

"Detective Petreski," the hairy vision growled. He must be a werewolf. The growly kind. I wished my instincts were more developed.

"I wish my instincts were more developed," I whispered to Don.

"You do not have any instincts," Don said in a flat voice. "You are not a werewolf."

I had read about werewolf detectives. Some of my favorite books were about werewolf detectives. Or sheriffs. Werewolf sheriffs were good, too.

They were always big and growly and protective. I bet Detective Petreski was protective. Right now he was giving me a funny look, though.

"Why's he looking at us like that?" I asked Don.

"Maybe you're his mate and he's pissed off that he got shafted by fate," Don deadpanned.

"That is *so* not funny."

"What the hell are you two going on about?"

"Nothing." Don said, just as I said, "Mates."

The werewolf detective sighed and turned to Don.

"You look like the smart one," he said.

"Hey!"

"God, I hope so," said Don.

"Hey!"

"Y'all gave your statements to one of the uniformed officers, right?"

"Yes."

"Here's my card." He started to hand the card to Don. I was too quick, though (maybe I did have lupine reflexes!) and snatched it from his hand. He growled again and snatched it back, handing it to Don. "You," he pointed at Don. "*You* call me if either of you thinks of anything else, got it?"

"Got it."

"Okay, smart one. Get your little friend home, make sure he's taking his meds, or whatever."

Detective Petreski turned his back on us and made his way down to where a woman in a jumpsuit was crouched next to the body.

"Okay, you heard the detective. Let's get you home, Wolf Man."

We walked to the western edge of the crime scene and ducked under the tape. A few people tried to ask us questions, but we ignored them and started walking faster. We were almost home when Don asked, "what the hell got into you back there?"

"What do you mean?" Because honestly, there were so many things he could have been asking about.

"When Detective Petreski came over. You were acting fairly normal, and then – boom – crazy werewolf Jake was back."

I shrugged. "I dunno. I took one look at him and all coherent thought went right out of my head."

"Ew."

"What?"

"Lust at first sight, then?"

"And how."

"Great. Now you're going to be mooning over some detective for weeks."

"What do you care?"

"Because I'll have to listen to you going on and on about him. And then you'll see him out somewhere with his wife or girlfriend and then I'll have to nurse you through your broken heart."

"You make me sound pathetic."

"You're not pathetic, Jake. But you do get carried away when you've got a crush. Try to rein it in this time."

"Fine. Whatever." We were standing outside our respective apartments now. I could see a tiny paw sticking out from under Don's door, trying to reach his foot. "You'd better get inside and deal with that," I said, pointing down and slipping into my apartment while Don was distracted.

Sure, I'd had disappointing crushes in the past, who hasn't? But I don't think I'd ever been as bad as Don made out. Besides, that was a long time ago and I wasn't a kid any more. And there was something different about Detective Petreski that I just couldn't put my finger on. I didn't have time to think about that now, though. I needed to get to class, and after that I had to go see Miss Nancy.

Jake Buys a Candle

MISS NANCY'S place was a bungalow on a quiet street near the farmer's market and botanica. It didn't look all that unusual from the outside. It was a little more colorful than its neighbors, and had more wind chimes around the porch, but there were no neon hands or tarot reader signs in the window. You had to know about Miss Nancy, and know how to find her.

I knew about her because she'd been my babysitter when I was a kid. I don't know how my parents knew her. For some reason I had never asked and had always just accepted Miss Nancy as a solid, if unusual, presence in my life.

I knocked on the door and turned to look around while I waited for her to come to the door. There had been a little gentrification up here, but nothing like the raping and pillaging that had been going on farther south where Clarence Wilson had been operating. The door opened, and Miss Nancy pushed open the screen door, motioning for me to come inside.

Miss Nancy always dressed like she was on her way to a Renaissance Festival. Her outfit today was bright purple, a long, drapey thing with swirling patterns and a matching turban. A couple of long dreadlocks hung down on one side, and she was wearing a purple lipstick the same shade as her outfit.

"Jake, honey! Come give me a big ol' hug!"

"Hi, Miss Nancy," I greeted her, giving her the bear hug I knew she'd expect. It always surprised me when I had to lean down to hug her. She had such a big personality, it seemed like she should be taller.

"Honey, you look like you've got the weight of the world on your shoulders."

"I feel better already, with one of your hugs, Miss Nancy. I like the lipstick, by the way."

"Shush. Come on through to the kitchen and we'll have some tea."

I sat at her kitchen table while she made the tea. I didn't ask what was in it – some blend of things she bought at the botanica, I assumed. Miss Nancy didn't do the cards and palms routine with me, although she did with others. But she told me once she only did it with them because they expected it and it relaxed them and let her see what she needed to see. Maybe because I'd known her most of my life, when I met with her we just chatted over a cup of tea in her kitchen.

She sat down at the table, the pot and cups between us, and studied my face. "You haven't been sleeping, have you?"

"Not well."

"Busy week."

"Weird week."

"Hmm." She poured us some tea and I started telling her what had been going on. All of it – the dreams, the kitten, everything I had told Don already, all about finding the body. I even told her about dreamy Detective Petreski. She nodded, and listened, and sipped her tea.

"Drink your tea, honey," was all she said when I finished. "You still got that squirrel visiting you?"

"Yeah. Why?"

"I think it's significant. I think that squirrel has something to reveal to you."

I wasn't so sure about that, but I wasn't going to argue with Miss Nancy.

"What about the dreams? And what happened after? You don't…" and now I was about to ask the thing I hadn't had the courage to bring up with Don. "You don't think I'm causing these things, do you?"

"Oh, honey, no! You're one of the kindest, gentlest souls I've even known. You'd never wish harm, real harm, on anybody, not even in your worst dreams."

I sighed and poured myself some more tea. "Then why is this happening now? To me? Have you ever heard of anything like this before?"

She sat back, folding her hands together in her lap and looking up towards the ceiling. I recognized her thinking pose and kept my mouth shut.

"Not exactly, no," she said after a minute, lowering her gaze back to meet mine. "Sometimes, when someone has the gift, it can manifest itself in strange and unsettling ways, but usually when someone's younger than you. Usually it happens during puberty."

"Well, I do seem to be stuck – I know Mom and Dad think I'm immature and don't want to grow up."

"This is not a joking matter, and you are not immature. Give me your hand."

She flipped my hand over and studied my palm for the first time in years – the last time I had been thirteen and freaking out over liking boys like I thought I should be liking girls.

"Maturity is not your problem, honey. You've just got too much going on in your head right now and it's keeping you from making a decision. Oh, and you're about to have a new presence in your life."

"A romantic presence?" I asked, thinking about Detective Petreski.

"Maybe. It's… complex. I have to think about this – this I *know* I haven't seen before."

I sighed. I knew there wouldn't be a simple answer.

"What about the dreams? I can't get a decent night's sleep. The nap I had yesterday was the first decent sleep I've had in days."

"After you found the kitten?"

I nodded.

"I think that's because you dreamed about it and resolved it. You saved that baby, and whatever… force… made you dream about it was quieted long enough for you to sleep. You were sleeping the sleep of the just, I'd say."

"But then… what about Wilton? That's a hell of a lot bigger than a tortured kitten. A man is dead. Will finding the body be enough? Is there more I have to do?"

"I don't know, honey. Like I said, I never saw anything like this before."

"I'm just so exhausted. I'd give anything for a good night's sleep."

She sat her tea cup down and stood slowly. "Jake, honey."

"Yes, Miss Nancy?" I looked up into her serious face.

"I've got something I think might help, but you have to promise me you'll never, ever, tell your mama I gave you this. You understand?"

I nodded. "Yes, ma'am."

She turned to open the freezer and took out a small baggie. I'd never tried marijuana before, but I knew that's what this was. "Oh, Miss Nancy, I'm not sure…"

"Honey, it won't hurt you none. If the dreams come back, just try a couple of puffs to mellow you out a little."

I tried to argue, but there's no arguing with Miss Nancy. It felt weird, letting my former babysitter give me pot, but I was desperate and took the two small joints.

"Now," Miss Nancy clapped her hands together, business as usual as if she hadn't just supplied me with a controlled substance, "are you going to drive me over to the market?" I always did when I came to visit. She wouldn't let me pay her, so I would drive her to the produce market, bakery, and botanica and help her carry her groceries.

Maybe this time I'd finally let her talk me into one of those candles she was always trying to get me to buy – Lucky in Love sounded appealing. You know, just in case.

Jake Annoys a Neighbor

I SLEPT a little better that night. I woke up a couple of times feeling lonely and confused and afraid, but I went right back to sleep. I had a feeling I knew what was going on, but my poor, tired brain wasn't ready to go there. Thank goodness I didn't have any morning classes this semester or I'd be toast.

Don knocked on my door around nine and I dragged myself out of bed to let him in.

"Are you just now getting up?" he asked.

I didn't answer and shut myself in the bathroom to perform my morning ablutions. When I came out, Don was standing in the kitchen doorway looking at the bright pink candle burning away on the stovetop.

"What the hell, dude? 'Bring Love to Me'?"

"Don't judge me. I've had a hard week. And I'm not the one carrying a cat around in a baby sling."

"We're bonding and building trust. And this way it'll be easier if I need to take him someplace in the future. This is practical."

I looked down at where Bridger's little face peeked out of the sling. He yawned and one front leg stretched out, toes spread and tiny claws extended. I sighed. I couldn't argue in the face of that level of cuteness.

"I'm guessing you want coffee?" I asked.

Don nodded, and since I was out of beans, we walked to Ground Up. Harry was working the counter as usual, and I could tell he was about to say something about animals in the shop when Don said, a tremor in his voice, "he's a rescue. He'd been tortured, and left to die and… and… he only has three legs!"

I was impressed by Don's blatant manipulation of the facts. Harry looked horrified and I thought he might burst into tears. Who knew Harry was such a soft touch when it came to animals? Don was obviously determined not to be separated from his new friend.

Harry gave us a French press on the house, I treated Don to a scone, in honor of his performance, and we settled onto a sofa in the corner to watch everyone come and go.

I saw the man I had seen at the park yesterday – the grim one with the bulldog. He was sitting at one of the outside tables with his dog. There was a woman with him. She was knitting, and every once in a while they'd say something to each other, but mostly he read a newspaper and she would talk to people as they passed or stopped by the table. She seemed to know a lot of people. I pointed them out to Don, but he was unimpressed.

I heard a deep, unmistakable voice drift around the corner. "Is there somewhere more private where we can talk?"

I grabbed Don's arm.

"Dude? What?"

"It's him! He's here!"

"Who?"

"The detective! My candle! It's working already!"

"Or maybe he's checking out leads in the area?"

I shook my head, my stomach fluttering. "Shh!"

He came around the corner, wearing a dark, tailored suit. If he saw us sitting on the sofa he didn't say anything. He waited for Harry to come out from behind the counter and they passed us as they went to the small storage room behind us. I knew she couldn't be far behind, but I still jumped when Detective Perez came around the corner. Her eyes narrowed when she saw us and she stopped as she passed.

"What are you doing here?" she asked, looking directly at me.

"Um, coffee?"

"Perez! Get in here!" I heard Detective Petreski call, and she moved on.

"She really -"

"Shh," I shushed Don again. "I want to listen."

"You can't do that! This is an official *murder* investigation!"

"Then go away, but I'm listening."

I knew Don was curious, too, because he shut up and we strained to hear what was being said. Bridger took a nap, so at least he was quiet.

The storage room had not been built for privacy, and being closer to the loose-fitting door I was able to hear most of what was being said.

"... same Harry Stiles arrested and charged with vandalism and assault in Austin in 1989?" That was Petreski.

"Yes, but -"

"And again in 1990, in Lubbock?"

"Yes, but I -"

"Have there been any more incidents since then?"

"No! Those were -"

"Were what?"

"Look, there was this girl..."

I heard Perez make a snorting sound before she said, "Yeah, isn't there always?"

"Look, I'm not saying it excuses what I did, but I was... we were toxic together, you know? I figured that out, broke it off, and kept out of trouble ever since. Not even a parking ticket, I swear."

There was silence for a few seconds, and then Perez asked, "Do you recognize this man?" They must have shown him a picture.

"Yeah. That's Clarence Wilton, right? They found him in the bayou yesterday?"

"Close enough," Petreski again. "He ever come in here?"

"Sometimes. I've seen him here before."

"Mornings or evenings?"

"I'm mostly here in the mornings, that's when I've seen him. You'd have to ask the evening staff if they've seen him."

"You ever talk to him?"

"I guess. Chit-chat at the counter, that kind of thing."

"Because, see," Perez jumped in, "someone saw you talking to him day before yesterday, out on the patio."

"Yeah, maybe. If I went out on the patio to check for cups or trash and he was out there, sure."

"Our source tells us you were arguing."

"Source?"

"Just answer Detective Perez, please, sir. Were you and Mr. Wilton arguing on the patio?"

I heard Harry take a deep breath and sigh. "I remember asking someone not to smoke a pipe out there. Did he smoke a pipe?"

I didn't hear the answer, but it must have been in the affirmative.

"Then that must have been it. There was a guy out there lighting up a pipe. We don't allow pipe or cigar smoking, so I asked him to put it out. He started complaining that no one else was out there so it should be okay. I told him rules are rules, we exchanged some words, and he left."

"Was he driving or walking, did you notice?"

"I didn't notice. He left and I got back to work. I didn't have time to think about him after that."

"And he was alone? You didn't see him talking to anyone?"

A moment of silence, Harry must have been thinking, and then, "No, not that I noticed."

"And where were you Tuesday night, between ten and midnight?" Perez's voice.

"At home, asleep. I have to get here by five to open up."

"Can anyone corroborate that?"

"No. I was alone."

"Would anyone notice if you left your place? Neighbor? Landlord?"

"Not that I know of."

Some more silence, and someone must have handed Harry a card. "Please call if you think of anything, and please don't leave town without speaking to one of us first."

As the detectives passed us on their way out, Petreski turned and looked at us. Bridger started to stir and the movement drew the detective's attention.

"He's a rescue," Don said, on the defensive. "He has special needs."

Petreski shook his head. "I'm not going to bust you over a kitten."

He turned to me, a puzzled look on his face, like he was trying to figure something out. I smiled, because he was awfully nice to look at and I wanted to appear friendly and approachable, which I am, actually, but he looked like he needed a nudge.

"Petreski!" Perez called from the door where she stood, tapping her foot. I had to say something, so I said the first thing that popped into my head.

"He was there. At the scene yesterday."

"Who? Harry?"

"No." I shook my head and pointed to the front window. "That man with the bulldog. He was standing on the hill, watching, and then he left."

"Do you know him?"

"No."

"Was he with anyone?"

"Not that I saw. A woman went up to him and said something, but he just shook his head and left."

"Okay. Thanks, uh..."

"Jake. Jake Hillebrand."

"Thanks, Mr. Hillebrand."

He turned to catch up to his partner, and on their way out he stopped to speak to the man with the bulldog. I didn't see what happened with that because Harry came out about then, looking shaken.

"You okay?" Don asked him.

"Huh? Sure. You guys need anything?"

We shook our heads, but Harry stayed where he was, and his eyes were drawn again to Don's baby sling.

"You wanna see him?" Don asked. Harry nodded and we shifted to make room for him on the sofa. Don opened the carrier and we all looked down to see Bridger, curled in a ball with his front paws crossed over his face. He stirred a little and stretched, and I'm sure the sight of three grown men mooning over a sleeping kitten was something to see.

Harry reached over to stroke Bridger's fur and I could feel some of the tension draining out of him. "I didn't know you were an animal lover," I said.

Harry nodded. "Yeah, that's what got me into trouble in the first place."

"Huh?"

"I know you must have heard – that –" he indicated the storage room with a jerk of his head. "I got involved with a couple of animal rights groups when I was in college. I hooked up with one of the girls in the group. You know how it is. Love makes you do stupid things sometimes."

"Yeah," Don and I said, in perfect harmony.

"Yeah. So we were picketing an animal lab and things got out of hand. After things went bad in Austin, we transferred to Texas Tech, but it was the same thing all over again. That's when I realized I needed to get out."

"But you did realize, and you did what you needed to do. Now you've got this place. Seems to me you've got your act together," I told him.

"I guess so. But every once in a while my past gets stirred up again."

Bridger was purring louder now, and rolled over to show us his belly. Harry give him a last scratch before standing up. "Okay, gotta get back to work. You can keep bringing him in, as long as he's in the sling. Just be discreet, okay?"

"Okay," Don agreed, and he wrapped Bridger back up as Harry headed towards the front. "How did he know?" Don said after a minute.

"How did who know what?"

"Detective Petreski? How did he know I had a kitten in here?"

"Maybe his tail was sticking out or something."

"No, he was all the way inside. How could he have known it was a kitten?"

"What else could it be?"

"All kinds of things. A puppy, a rabbit, a guinea pig."

"He's a detective, right? He's got all kinds of training and skills, probably. Or maybe he just guessed and didn't care if he got it right or not."

"Maybe."

"You. You were at the crime scene yesterday."

I looked up to see the man I had pointed out to Detective Petreski standing over me. I glanced out the window to see the knitting woman holding her bag in one hand, the dog's leash in the other, and watching us, her face looking pinched.

"Um, yeah?"

"What did you tell that cop?" I shifted my gaze back to him. He looked angry – his face was red, his jaw thrust forward, even the little alligator on his green polo shirt seemed to vibrate with rage.

"I didn't –"

"I saw him in here talking to you. Then he starts asking me questions. What did you tell him?"

"I was there. He asked me to tell him if I remembered anything, and I remembered seeing you in the crowd, so I told him I saw you. That's it."

His hands clenched into fists, and for a second I thought he might hit me. I wasn't afraid, really – he wasn't young and had the physique of a man who spent all day in a desk chair. I was younger, fitter, and a fast runner, but I was sunk in a low-slung sofa that would be hard to get out of and I didn't want Don and Bridger getting hurt.

"Look, lots of people were there, you obviously live in the neighborhood, so there's no reason for you not to be there, too, right? It's a good place to walk your dog." I glanced back out to where his companion waited, looking more agitated now. I really hoped she wasn't concerned because this guy had a violent temper.

Maybe he'd been taking anger management courses. He closed his eyes, and I could see his lips move as he counted or talked himself down. After a few seconds he opened his eyes. He was still glaring at me, but his hands relaxed and he rolled his shoulders. "Just stay away from me and out of my business. Got it?"

I nodded, and he spun on his heel and stormed out of the shop. A few heads turned to watch him pass, and then things went back to normal.

Harry stuck his head out from the serving area. "You guys okay?"

We nodded and Harry went back to work.

"I think I've had enough excitement for one morning," Don said.

"Yeah, me too. But I don't want to bump into that guy outside. Let's give it a few minutes before we leave."

We finished our coffee and bussed our dishes. Don went on outside because Bridger was starting to get fidgety and he didn't want to push his luck with Harry. I stopped by the service window to thank Harry for the coffee again.

"It's cool, man. You sure you're okay? Mr. Katz is, well, he can have a temper."

"Yeah, fine. Is that who that was? I didn't know his name."

"Yeah, Josh Katz. He's president of one of the local preservation groups. He's kind of a regular here, but usually in the afternoon. Just FYI, in case you want to steer clear of him."

"Thanks. We'll keep it in mind."

I caught up with Don outside and we waited for a break in the traffic so we could cross the street.

"What were you talking to Harry about?"

"He told me a little about that guy. His name is Josh Katz and – get this – he's the head of a preservation group in the neighborhood!"

"So?"

"So, think about it. A guy with a temper, gung-ho about preserving the character of the neighborhood? Takes his dog for a walk and bumps into Clarence Wilton on a dark, empty trail?"

"You're not seriously saying you think he killed Wilton?"

"It's a theory."

"It's wild speculation."

"Do you think we should call Detective Petreski?"

"No! You put Katz on his radar. If there's a connection, he'll find it. Stay out of it, Jake."

I stepped over some tree roots that had broken through the sidewalk and focused on navigating the chunks of concrete. I looked up and saw a "For Sale" sign halfway down the block. Another bungalow, likely to be bought by a developer and torn down or moved. Every bungalow gone was another rip in the fabric of the neighborhood – it was unraveling before our eyes and a part of me sympathized with the thought of someone driven to violence to stop it.

"What is it?" Don had moved a few feet ahead of me and turned back to see what was keeping me.

"It could have been anyone."

"You're talking about Wilton?"

"Yeah. Half the people in this neighborhood are probably nursing champagne hangovers this morning. Can you think of anyone they'd rather see dead?"

"A few elected officials spring to mind."

"But how many of them walk their dog on the bayou trails at night?"

"What you're saying is that there's no shortage of motive or opportunity in the area."

"Yeah."

"But how was he killed? You said you smelled blood. Did you hear a gunshot? None was reported – it would have been all over the message board if there had. You can't fart walking down the street here without someone reporting you for firing off a bazooka at the middle school."

"I didn't hear anything like that. Stabbed, I guess?"

"I know we've got some gun nuts in the neighborhood. I'm sure they take their precious weapons with them when they walk in the park. But who walks around with a knife? If he was shot, it could be a crime of opportunity, or passion."

"But a stabbing… yeah, no one just walks around with a knife, as far as I know. To meet up with him on the trail, and have a knife handy… that would have to be planned. Someone who knows him, knows his schedule? Lying in wait for him?"

"Or someone who does wander around with a knife, and Wilton stumbled across him."

I didn't like the implications of that. "You're talking about some psycho with a knife. That maybe Wilton was a victim of opportunity, not a target, and anyone and everyone could be in danger."

"Yeah."

"Fuck."

We started walking again.

"Where did you get a baby sling, anyway?" I asked.

"I made it out of an old sheet."

"Of course you did."

"Power of the internet, dude."

"Yeah." I was still thinking about Wilton, and whether he was convenient or a target. If I had bad dreams tonight, they might have a whole new cause.

Boo Barges In

I TRIED to put aside my gloomy thoughts for a few hours and get through class and homework and dinner. Don was off tonight, so didn't ask me to watch Bridger for him. He'd suggested watching a movie, but I needed to study and I needed to think. The whole thing with the dreams and Wilton was doing a real number on my head and I thought maybe, if I could have one quiet hour with no interruptions, I could reach some kind of clarity. Or take a nap. I'd settle for either at this point.

I had just settled into a corner of the sofa with a notepad and a pencil when I heard a scratching at the door. I had been thinking about knife-wielding maniacs all day, so my initial response was a squeak and my pencil flew across the room.

There was about a one-inch gap between the bottom of the door and the floor, and I could see a shadow there. Moving as quietly as I could, I crossed the room, then crouched down to look under the door. A bright green eye looked back at me, surrounded by black fur. A cat. I tried to remember whether any of my neighbors had a black cat, but came up blank. It was still looking at me, and then it stuck one of its front legs under the door, straining towards me, and meowed.

"You want in, kitty?" I asked.

Another meow. I guessed that was a yes. I decided a cat was probably harmless compared to a knife-wielding maniac, and stood to open the door.

When I opened the door the cat rolled to its feet and craned its neck to look inside. "Come on, then," I coaxed, and it entered, fluffy tail held high.

He (I checked) was gorgeous – fluffy, shiny, jet black coat, bright green eyes, and when I picked him up he was solid muscle. This was no stray – this was someone's well-cared-for darling.

"Now where did you come from, hmm? No collar. You got a microchip? Huh?" He melted into me and started to purr, so I didn't have the heart to put him down. I walked around the apartment holding him. We looked out all the windows, and I took him in the kitchen and fixed him a bowl of water. "You want some water? Huh, Boo-Boo Kitty? You want some water?" Crap, I was already talking baby-talk and naming the furry intruder.

I finally plopped him onto the sofa and went across the landing to knock on Don's door.

"What's up?" he asked when he answered.

"Come check this out." He followed me back across the landing and we stood in the door of my apartment, looking at my visitor, blinking back at us from the arm of the sofa.

"You got a cat?"

"No. He just showed up and, like, knocked on the door. Isn't he gorgeous?"

"You gonna keep him?"

"I can't keep him. He's gotta be someone's pet. Do you think we should introduce him to Bridger?"

"Too late for that." We looked down to see that Bridger had followed Don across the landing to see what was going on. He hop-limped towards the sofa and my visitor jumped down to approach the little fluff-ball. We watched, ready to intervene, as the big black cat circled Bridger, sniffing at him and nudging at the spot where his fourth leg should be.

Bridger swatted at the bigger cat, and knocked himself over. I stifled a laugh and Don jabbed me with an elbow.

Boo – it popped out earlier and I had to call him something – head butted the kitten, then picked him up by the scruff of the neck and took him to the sofa. "Hey! No!" I called and headed towards them.

"No," Don laid a hand on my arm. "It's okay."

We walked over to stand behind the sofa and looked down to see Boo, holding Bridger down with one paw and licking furiously at his face. Both cats were purring, and we figured they were getting along okay and left them to it to get beers for ourselves.

We watched the cats bathing for a while, until Bridger got bored and wanted to play. Boo tolerated him, and twitched his tail back and forth for the youngster to chase. After a while, though, Boo gave Bridger a little slap-down and headed to the other end of the sofa, where I was sitting.

"Hey, Boo," I said. "You looking for a lap?"

He meowed, and climbed aboard. After circling a couple of times he flopped down and closed his eyes.

"That's the damndest thing," Don said.

"I know, right? Where did he come from? How did he show up at my door? So weird."

"If you keep him you'll need to get him fixed, you know."

I felt Boo stiffen in my lap. He must have been responding to my own unease. "I'm not keeping him. He's not my cat, so it's not my decision. He's full grown, and look how gorgeous he is. What if he's, like, a champion stud or something? His bits are staying where they are."

Boo stretched and started purring again, and I stroked that soft, shiny fur. He was probably the most beautiful cat I'd ever seen.

"Okay," Don said. "Well, I'm off. Come on Bridger, let's go home." Don scooped up his three-legged terror and headed back to his own place. I got up to close the door and turned to see Boo watching me from the sofa.

"Time for me to get to bed, Boo-Boo Kitty. What'll it be? In or out?" He didn't move, so I gave him one more chance. "You wanna go home, Boo?" He blinked and jumped down from the sofa, but instead of heading for the door he jumped up onto the bed and started sniffing around.

"Okay, then. I'll leave this window open, though, in case you want to leave or go take care of your business. I don't have a litter box, Boo, so be a gentleman, okay?"

He blinked at me again, so I opened the window and crossed my fingers. I rattled around the apartment for a while, cleaning up and getting ready for bed. Boo was still stretched out across the bed and I had to shove him to one side to make room for myself. "Don't be a bed hog, Boo," I told him as I slipped under the covers. I rolled onto my side and reached over to turn off the bedside lamp. Boo curled up against my belly and I hoped I didn't scare him off with any bad dreams.

Of course the dreams came. I started to feel panicky and confused. I was in a familiar place, but it felt wrong. I went from room to room, searching for what was missing. The Jake part of my brain knew what was wrong, but the dream me was confused and lonely. My dream-self started to whimper and cry, and then I was being shaken awake.

I gasped and clutched my chest, feeling fur. I've got a little chest hair, but not that much, and I had put a t-shirt on before going to bed. Boo. I pulled my hand away, not wanting to hurt or scare him. He was kneading at my chest and purring, and I realized that was what had woken me.

"Oh… oh geez. Did you wake me up, Boo? Did I scare you?" There was a little light coming in from the streetlight outside and I could make out Boo's shape in the bed next to me. I scratched the ruff around his neck and he head-butted my chest. "Sorry, Boo. It's okay, just a bad dream. You may want to go home, you know. I get a lot of those."

Boo head-butted me again and made a mournful little trilling sound.

"Yeah, Boo. It's pretty sad, huh? Not much fun to sleep with. Shit. I hadn't thought about that. If I ever did get that hot detective to notice me, it wouldn't get very far. Nobody wants to sleep with someone who wakes up screaming or crying every few minutes."

Boo made that trilling sound again and started rubbing on me. He head-butted my chin and it was strangely comforting.

"You're so sweet, Boo. I wish I could keep you and you could be my kitty. Someone's probably really missing you right now. But maybe you could stay a little longer, huh?"

Boo collapsed against me and started purring again.

"Good decision, Boo."

Pancakes and Petreski

BOO WAS gone in the morning. I had expected that, but I missed him anyway and wondered whether he would come back. Last night was the best night's sleep I'd had in a few days, and I had a feeling Boo was a contributing factor.

But a more pressing concern at the moment was that with all the excitement the last few days, I still hadn't made it to the grocery store and I wanted pancakes for breakfast.

"Don?" I knocked on his door. "You up?"

I heard some shuffling noises, and then Don opened the door. He was dressed, but still looking bleary-eyed. Pre-coffee, then.

"I want pancakes."

He blinked at me.

"Pancakes. I'm going to get some? Do you want to go?"

He scratched his chest and blinked again. "Yeah. Okay. Where?"

I knew he was asking because he wanted to go somewhere walking distance. He didn't have a car, and didn't like my driving. I didn't blame him. The only thing worse than my driving is my parking. He probably wanted to bring Bridger, too, which meant someplace with a patio. "Onion Creek?"

"Give me a second." He left the door open, and I watched while he set up the baby sling – I guess I should start calling it the cat sling – and got Bridger settled into it. He tucked one of the catnip toys in there and stuffed his wallet into his pocket.

"What are you going to do when he's too big for the sling?" I asked as we started walking.

"Even full-grown he won't be bigger than a baby. But I've also been thinking about training him to walk on a leash."

"You can do that with cats?"

"Yeah. Need to start him young, though. You seem more with it this morning."

"Finally got a decent night's sleep."

"No dreams?"

"One, but Boo woke me up and we cuddled and I didn't have any more."

"Boo? The cat? He stayed?"

"Yeah. But I left a window open and he was gone when I woke up this morning."

"Don't feed him or he'll never leave."

I didn't say anything.

"You're totally thinking about feeding him now, aren't you?"

I shrugged. We had reached the intersection and I pushed the button for the walk signal.

"You said it yourself, he's not your cat."

The little man lit up and we started crossing the street.

"Jake…"

"I'm not going to feed him, but I can think about it. It just felt so good having him there."

"Maybe you should get a cat, then?"

"I'll think about it." But I didn't think that was the answer. Not exactly. I didn't tell Don I had left the window open, in case Boo came back. I hoped the squirrel didn't decide to explore the great indoors while I was out, but that didn't seem like his style.

Don settled at a table on the patio while I went inside to place our orders. When I came back out with our coffee there was a girl leaning over his chair, cooing over Bridger, so I hung back for a minute. When she headed back to her own table and her three giggling friends I rolled my eyes and reclaimed my seat.

"That kitten is a total chick magnet."

"I can't afford to date right now, you know that."

"Geez, when girls see that furry little face and find out he's only got three legs, they'll be buying *you* dinner. Girls love that stuff."

"Since when are you an expert on women?"

"I'm an observer of the human condition."

"Yeah? Observe this." He picked up his coffee mug with his middle finger extended.

"Very classy."

We were making good headway on our pancakes when a shadow fell across the table. I raised my head and almost choked when I saw Detective Petreski looking down at us.

"Gentlemen," he drawled as he pulled out a chair and sat, unbuttoning his suit jacket. I caught a glimpse of the shoulder holster he wore, and suppressed a shudder. I hated guns, but for some reason the thought of the leather holster under that stylish jacket was turning my crank.

We sat, looking at him but not saying anything. Don chewed, and I took a sip of coffee. Why was he here? Sitting with us? Bridger chose that moment to stir, sticking his head out and yawning. Detective Petreski looked down at the kitten, and Don broke the silence.

"It's a pet-friendly patio."

"I told you yesterday, I'm not going to bust your chops over a kitten. Especially not one with 'special needs'."

Was it my imagination, or did he seem a little friendlier today? Maybe he was a cat lover? I looked around, but didn't see Perez anywhere.

"We need to talk," he said after a minute.

"About what?" I finally found my voice.

He turned to look at me, and I forced myself to sit still under that bright green gaze.

"A variety of things. First of all, why didn't you tell us that Thomas Wilton is a classmate of yours?"

"Thomas Wilton?"

"Clarence Wilton's son. You have a class together. Why didn't you tell anyone?"

"I didn't know. I don't know him. What class?"

"American History."

"Geez. That's a huge class, I don't know everyone in there. That must be why he looked familiar. I couldn't place him, though. I wasn't hiding anything, I swear."

He kept looking at me, and it was on the verge of feeling awkward when he nodded and turned to Don.

"Mister Olson, may I ask how you acquired your feline companion?"

"Huh?"

"He wants to know how you got Bridger."

"Yes, thank you, I knew what he meant." Don looked at me for a minute, and I shrugged. The crazy might as well get out there – either Petreski could handle it or not.

"We found him," Don said.

"Where? And how?"

"The old trestle bridge over the bayou. The bike path. Someone, we think maybe some kids, had put him in a bag and hung it from the bridge. They just…" Don pressed Bridger against his chest. "They just left him there, scared and alone."

Petreski's jaw was tight, his lips pressed in a thin line. I wouldn't want to be one of those kids if Petreski ever caught up with them. "When was this?"

"Tuesday morning."

"That makes two mornings in a row you made grim discoveries along the bayou."

"Bridger had a better ending," I said.

"Yes," Petreski turned to me. "But what I'm wondering is, what led you to discover the kitten in the first place. Is the bridge a regular walk for you?"

Don and I looked at each other.

"No," I answered.

"Jake had a dream."

I closed my eyes so I wouldn't have to see Petreski's face when he decided I was some kind of nut case.

"What kind of dream?"

"A bad one," I answered, not opening my eyes.

"He dreamed he was a werewolf."

"What is it with you and werewolves?" Petreski asked.

"There's no such thing as werewolves," I said, surprising them both into silence.

Don was the first to recover. "Then why…?"

I opened my eyes. "Because joking about something so… out there… was easier than admitting that something really weird was happening. That maybe I really was losing it."

"You're not losing it."

I turned to Petreski. "How can you be so sure?"

"I know what losing it looks like - I see it often enough in my work. I don't know what is going on, but you're not losing it."

"I think he's a psychic."

Petreski and I turned to look at Don. "What?" he said, looking back and forth between us.

"Tell me about this dream," Petreski said, turning back to me.

"Tell him, Jake."

It's a hard thing to do, spilling your guts about your special kind of crazy to someone you barely know – especially when you're attracted to them and want them to think you're amazing. I had to give him credit, though. He didn't bat an eye, and he didn't act like I was a lunatic. He wanted us to show him where we found Bridger, but he let us finish our breakfast first. All in all, he was pretty cool about the whole thing, which didn't help cure my crush and I'm sure Don despaired for the future state of my heart.

We were standing on the trestle bridge, looking east towards where Wilton had been found. Don had taken Bridger onto the grass to let him stretch his legs and see if he needed to pee. Petreski turned to watch Bridger hop around in the weeds. "That is one very lucky kitten."

"Don is besotted," I said, looking along the edge of the bayou to see if there were any birds today.

"Tell me about Wilton."

"You've seen my statement, right?"

"Yeah, but tell me what's not in your statement. It was another dream, right? Like the one that brought you here?"

I nodded, feeling queasy again as I remembered how I felt coming out of that dream. "Only, like, a hundred times worse."

"Tell me."

I told him everything I could remember, even about throwing up. He was silent when I finished, his gaze fixed in the distance.

"Am I in trouble? For not putting this in my statement? I mean, it makes me look crazy, right? Or guilty? Crazy is better, I guess, but –"

He silenced me with a hand on my shoulder. "It's okay."

"It is?"

"Yeah." He let go of my shoulder and turned back to look out over the bayou again. "I get it. Look, Mr. Hillebrand… Jake?" I nodded. "I have a higher tolerance for… the unusual… than some of my colleagues, but even I might have found it suspicious without some context."

"Context?"

"Just don't talk to anyone else about this for now, okay?"

"Okay. Sure." I turned to see Don walking towards us, Bridger back in his sling with his head sticking out, gaze fixed on Petreski.

"Hey, little guy," Petreski said, reaching out to scratch Bridger's head with one finger. Bridger turned to rub his face on it, and Petreski chuckled when Bridger started licking with his tiny pink tongue. "They're so cute at this age."

"They're nice when they're older, too," I said, thinking of Boo.

Petreski turned to me and smiled. "Yes. Yes they are. Gentlemen, I need to get going. Are you okay to get home?"

We nodded and he left us there on the bridge. I watched him walk away, admiring the way he moved until Don elbowed me. I really needed to break him of that habit; I was starting to get bruises.

"Ow. What?"

"Stop ogling the detective."

"I wasn't ogling," I lied.

"Come on, let's head home. Don't you have an exam tomorrow?"

"Yeah, okay." I let Don lead me home, but I was still thinking about Petreski, and about how, maybe, he didn't think I was crazy.

❧

I spent most of the afternoon studying. I was kind of stressed out about my history midterm, so Don didn't ask me to watch Bridger while he went to work. Seriously, he's a cat, he doesn't need babysitting. I toyed with the idea of taking my books and laptop over to Ground Up for a while that afternoon, but I remembered what Harry had said about Josh Katz being an afternoon regular and I didn't want to bump into him.

I managed to put together a sad little bachelor meal from the bits and pieces in my kitchen, then took a long, hot shower. I had left a window open all day, just in case, but it turned out Boo was a more formal kind of cat. A little after nine I heard a scratching sound and a black paw curled under the door, announcing Boo's presence.

It was ridiculous to be so happy to see a cat – especially someone else's cat – but I rushed to open the door and scoop him up.

"Boo! You came back!" I buried my face in his neck and he purred like he was happy to see me, too.

I closed and locked the door without putting him down.

"Don't worry, Boo. The window is open in case you need to leave. Ooh, you smell so good!"

Boo wiggled a little and I put him down on the sofa.

"I've got to make it an early night, Boo. Not a lot of time to visit today. I have an exam tomorrow. Yeah, I know, what's an exam, right? It's okay, Boo-Boo Kitty." I reached over to rub his ears. "You don't need to know."

"I'm going to fix you a bowl of water, okay? But Don says I'd better not feed you or you'll never leave. Is that true?" I sighed and leaned over to kiss the top of his silky head. "Because if it's true I sure would be tempted to try it."

I put the bowl of water on the floor in the kitchen and started getting ready for bed. Boo watched me from his perch on the back of the sofa until I climbed into bed, and then trotted over to join me.

"So what's the deal, huh Boo? You don't like sleeping alone?" I rubbed him until he was stretched out long, and I could feel the vibration of his purring. "That's cool. Okay, hopefully I'll get a good night's sleep again, 'cause I've got a big exam tomorrow. Yeah – history, not my best subject. Get this, Boo. Turns out there's a guy in my class who is the son of a guy who was murdered the other day and… wait for it… I found the body. Yeah, I know. Pretty crazy, huh?"

Boo rolled over and fixed me with his bright green gaze. He was an excellent listener. "I know! I didn't even realize. I probably never would have known if that handsome detective hadn't told me. You remember, the one I told you about?"

Boo trilled and head-butted my hand.

"Yeah. I saw him again today. Don't judge me, Boo, but there's just something about him that feels like… like it fits. I know, I know, it's stupid. And Don's probably right, and I'm going to find out that I'm crushing on a straight guy and get my heart broken again, but there's no harm in a little daydreaming, right?"

Boo twisted around until he was looking at me upside down. He batted at my chin with one gentle paw, and I pulled him close against my chest. "You'd like him, Boo. He likes cats."

I was so tired it didn't take me long to fall asleep. It didn't take long for the dreams to start, either. It started out like the night before, feeling lonely, sad, and confused. That was bad enough, but this time I was frightened as well, and I felt helpless. I felt like crying, but tried to look around and figure out where I was. It was dark, and everything looked hard and angular, like boxes or cabinets. That was no help. I started to panic, and that was when Boo woke me up, purring and kneading my chest like he had the night before.

I lay there, tangled in the sheets and looking up at the ceiling, with Boo head-butting my cheek, and decided it was time to try something different. I turned to nuzzle Boo and gave him a few strokes. "Thanks, Boo. You're like, the best cat ever."

I got up and headed into the kitchen for a glass of water. Boo followed me and took a few dainty laps at his bowl. I downed about half of the glass, pulled a box of matches from the drawer and sat it on the counter next to the glass, then turned to open the freezer. I took out the baggie Miss Nancy had given me, and put that on the counter, too. I turned to look at Boo, who was watching from the floor.

"Miss Nancy said it might help repress the dreams, Boo. I really need a good night's sleep tonight." I turned back to look at the bag. "I've never even smoked a cigarette, Boo. I'll probably burn the house down trying to light it."

Boo yowled at me from the floor. It sounded like he didn't think this was a good idea, either.

"I'm desperate, Boo." He yowled again and rubbed up against my leg. "Yeah, I know. Sorry, Boo. You're about to witness the start of my life of crime, I suppose. Don't tell anyone, okay?"

I looked down. Boo was sitting, straight and tall, looking up at me. He gave me a tiny little mew, and his sharp teeth were a vivid white flash against his black fur.

I frowned, and took one of the joints out of the baggie. I resealed the bag, and put it back in the freezer. I held the hand-rolled cigarette up to my nose and sniffed. "Ew. That smells awful. People smoke this for fun, Boo. I don't know why."

I put one end in my mouth and struck one of the wooden matches against the side of the box. So far, so good, I thought as it caught and started to flame. It took a few tries, and two more matches, but I finally got the damn thing lit. I tried inhaling, and coughed at the burning, smoky feeling. "So not fun," I gasped, reaching for the water and gulping at it.

I gave it a few more tries, but as it hurt and burned less, I started feeling sick to my stomach. "Stay here, Boo. You don't need to see this." I staggered to the bathroom and promptly up-chucked into the toilet. I stood there, bent over and spitting, and realized I was still holding the joint. I tossed it in after my dinner and flushed the whole lot away.

I rinsed my mouth and brushed my teeth, and turned to see Boo watching me from the doorway. "I don't think I'm cut out to be a stoner, Boo." He squinted his eyes at me, which I had learned was a good thing, and meowed. I guess he approved. "Let's go back to bed. I'll just have to hope for the best."

For whatever reason the rest of my night was uneventful, and just like the day before, Boo was gone when I woke up. Fortunately I was feeling no ill effects from my smoking attempt, other than being hungrier than usual because I'd lost my dinner. I decided that my good night's sleep was down to Boo being there, because nothing that made me feel as wretched as smoking that joint could possibly have a positive effect. I'd give the other one back to Miss Nancy the next time I visited her.

Talking to Tom

I LOOKED around the full classroom – one of those auditorium-style rooms with tiers of seats sloping up to the doors in the back. I realized I was older than most of the students – I had put off taking this core class as long as I could. I wondered whether Thomas Wilton would be here for the exam. Didn't you get some kind of break or dispensation or something if you had a death in the family? I had heard that if your roommate died during the semester you got an automatic 4.0 and didn't have to take exams. I didn't know if that was true or not, but had always assumed it must be some kind of urban legend.

I scanned the upper rows and was surprised to see Wilton sitting, alone, on the back row. We were seated alphabetically, so that made sense. He looked up and our eyes met. I could tell when he recognized me, because his eyes got perfectly round, something I had never seen in real life. The instructor walked in at that point, and I turned to face the front of the room. So Wilton hadn't known we were classmates, either, I guessed. Small world, but that was Houston for you.

The exam was just as miserable as I had expected, but I was prepared and it was multiple choice, and that always worked in my favor. Afterwards, I stood outside the building, blinking in the sun and waiting for my weird post-test rush to settle down. I heard a throat clear to my left and wasn't surprised to see Wilton standing there.

"Hey," he said, shifting his weight and hiking his backpack up higher onto his shoulder.

"Hey. I didn't realize…"

"Yeah. Me neither." His eyes shifted back and forth before he looked at me again. "I don't know if it's okay for me to talk to you or not."

"I don't know. Probably not."

"Yeah, right," he said, but didn't move away.

"I was surprised to see you here today."

His expression changed, and he looked hard and angry for a second. "I can't put my life on hold because… well… it was a shock and all, but…" He let the thought drift off and shrugged.

I think he was trying to tell me that his father's death hadn't been the blow one would expect.

"Still, it must be tough. Sorry."

He shrugged again. "Okay. Anyway, I saw you in there and I wanted to, well, I don't know. It just seemed like I should say something. I mean, it would be weirder not to, don't you think?"

"Maybe. I guess."

"And, well, maybe…" he looked around again, and I noticed the crowds had dispersed and there were only a few other people around. "Maybe if we don't talk about… you know, *that*, it would be okay if I talked to you."

"Um, sure. I guess that would be okay."

"Cool. So, um, I was going to go get some lunch. You wanna…?" He gestured over his shoulder towards the food court. I wasn't sure I wanted to have lunch with him – it seemed like something Detective Petreski wouldn't approve of. But I had some questions that needed answers.

It was a little on the late side for lunch, so the lines weren't bad and there were plenty of tables and we could have an actual conversation. I needed to know, and since it wasn't directly about *that*, I figured it wouldn't be strange for me to ask about Murphy, since I had found him and turned him over to Tom, as he told me he preferred to be called

"Murphy? He's been acting strange, but that's to be expected, right? I mean he was really Dad's dog. They were practically inseparable."

"I've heard that animals experience grief and loss."

"Yes. Exactly. That's exactly what it seems like. It seems to get worse in the evening, and I'm the only one who can get near him anymore. I wonder if that's because I smell more like Dad or something? I don't know how that stuff works."

I didn't, either, but what I had been experiencing seemed, mostly, to fit with the grief theory.

"Mom's freaking out, though."

"Like, with grief?"

"Hah! Funny. No. About Murphy. He's been acting out and snapping. She wants to get rid of him. But he was Dad's dog, and Dad was an asshole, but Murphy's just, well, sad, you know?"

I nodded. I knew.

"So, I think Murphy just needs some time to grieve and then he'll be better. He's a good dog."

"You want to keep him."

"Yeah, I guess I do." Tom smiled a little at that. "You're pretty smart, huh?"

I shrugged.

Disengaging from Tom took another half hour. I got the impression that he didn't have many people to talk to, and the way he was smiling at me before I left made me uncomfortable. He seemed nice, and he wasn't bad looking, but I was *so* not going there, even if I hadn't set my sights on a certain detective.

❧

"I need Detective Petreski's card!" I called as I knocked on Don's door.

"And hello to you, too," Don greeted me as he opened the door.

"Sorry, hi. But I really need that card."

"He said *I* should call him, remember?"

"If *either* of us think of something. I need to talk to him!"

"Okay then, fine. Come in and I'll call him. It better be the real deal, though, not some flaky excuse."

"It's real. Hurry."

Don turned his back on me while he dialed - where was the trust? Petreski must have picked up right away, and it was frustrating to only hear one side of the conversation.

"Um, hello, Detective Petreski? This is Don Olson… Yeah, the one with the kitten. You gave me your card and said I should call you if my friend or I thought of anything… No, I didn't. Jake did. He said he needed to talk to you… Yes, he's here." Don passed the phone to me. "Here."

I pressed the phone to my ear. "Hello?" I said, sitting on Don's sofa. Don sat at the other end, listening and dangling a string for Bridger.

"Hello, Jake?"

"Yeah. Look, I don't know if it's important, but I think it's the kind of thing I should tell you about…"

"Okay, what is it?"

"Well, I had my history midterm today…"

"Oh, well, that *is* important." What the? Sarcasm?

"History as in the class I have with Tom Wilton."

"Thomas Wilton? So it's Tom now, is it?" he asked with an edge in his voice. That was more like it.

"That's what I'm trying to tell you if you'd give me a chance."

There was silence for a moment and then, "Sorry. Go ahead."

Wow, easy as that? Okay. "So, I was looking around the room before class, and Wilton was there. He saw me, and he looked really surprised, so I guess he didn't know we were in the same class, either. Anyway, after the exam was over he came up to me and started talking."

"Did he try to talk to you about the case?"

"Not really. I said we shouldn't, and he said maybe it would be okay to talk as long as we didn't talk about that, and I couldn't think of a reason why not. And he seemed really lonely and wanted someone to eat lunch with, so I did."

"You had lunch with him?"

"Well, not like a date or anything, although I do think he might have been trying to flirt with me at the end, there."

"Don't flirt with Tom Wilton, or anyone else connected to the case. Technically you are all still suspects until you've been cleared."

"Suspects? Does that… does that mean *I'm* a suspect, too?"

"Technically. Was there anything else, or were you just calling to dish about your conquest?"

"Wow. Snarky! Yes, actually. We didn't talk about the case, but I asked about Murphy. I mean, that seemed like a natural thing to do, since I found him and, well, you know the other part. But he dropped a couple of zingers about his relationship with his dad, and about his mom."

"Such as?"

"Well, the fact that he was back at school already should be a clue, but he basically told me he wasn't losing any sleep over his dad's death. Neither is his mom, if I understood correctly. He called his dad an asshole at one point."

"And Murphy?" I decided to forgive the snark since he seemed genuinely concerned about the dog.

"Practically prostrated by grief. Not handling it well. Acting out, and Tom's mom is threatening to get rid of him."

"And this fits with… you know?"

"Yeah," I said, nodding even though I knew he couldn't see me.

"Okay. You did the right thing calling me. And stay away from Tom Wilton."

"I'll try, but we're in the same class and I think he wants to be friends or something."

"Just do your best."

Don was watching me as I disconnected the call and put his phone down on the cushion between us.

"Sounds like you've had quite a day," he said.

"Yeah."

"Wanna go over to Ground Up and have a beer on the patio? Good weather for it."

I looked at the phone. Three o'clock. "Maybe just one. But if Katz is there, you have to block him while I make a run for it."

I dumped my messenger bag in my apartment and washed up while Don got Bridger loaded into his cat sling

We found a sunny spot on the patio, and got a couple of happy hour specials. I didn't have class again until Monday, and I was determined to relax and try not to think about anything unpleasant.

"So," Don paused to take a sip of his beer. "Tell me about young Tom Wilton trying to pick you up."

I sighed. So much for good intentions. "He did not try to pick me up. I think he's just lonely. And you heard what I told Petreski."

"Yeah, but I want details."

"No."

"You told Petreski," Don pouted.

"That was reporting facts to an officer of the law as they pertain to an ongoing criminal investigation."

"What the wha…?"

"You heard me. Giving you details would just be, well…"

"Confiding in your best friend?"

"Gossip."

"Oh, well."

"So when are you going to start training the tiny terror to use a leash?"

"He needs to get a little bigger first, and stronger."

I closed my eyes and soaked up some sunshine while I listened to Don rattle on about how to leash train cats. It wasn't completely boring, and I grunted and asked questions in appropriate places.

We had exhausted that topic of conversation and I was contemplating a second beer, when someone approached our table.

"Excuse me?"

I looked up to see the lady who had been sitting with Josh Katz the other morning. I looked around to see if he was anywhere in sight before turning back to her.

"Um, I'm alone. My husband isn't here today," she said.

"Oh, ah, that's not…"

"It's okay," she said. "I know Josh can be, well, abrasive. That's why I came over. I wanted to apologize about that."

"Well, thanks, but does he know you're apologizing for him?"

She blushed, and looked down at the bag she was holding. It was some kind of open-topped canvas tote filled with yarn and sticks – knitting needles, I remembered. My mother had once tried knitting for about twenty minutes. I come by my indecision naturally.

"No, he doesn't. But I know he was dreadfully unfair to you, and he'll never apologize. I just wanted to say something to you. He's not a bad man, you see. He's just very passionate about the neighborhood, and sometimes his emotions get the better of him."

"Look, Mrs. Katz, is it?"

She nodded, "Jennifer."

"Look, Jennifer. You seem really nice, and I'm sorry you felt like you needed to come over and apologize. I love our neighborhood too, but I didn't appreciate being the target of misdirected anger and threats. Your husband asked me to stay away from him, and I'm happy to oblige as much as I can, but I'm not going to go out of my way or change my lifestyle. Do you think that's going to be a problem for him?"

"I don't know, to be perfectly honest."

"Okay, well I appreciate your honesty. Oh!" I stopped her as she turned to leave. "I was wondering – there was this lady I saw at the crime scene the other day, and I wondered whether you know her? She was probably in her forties, short blonde hair, slim. Not real tall, and wearing jeans and a dark blue sweatshirt. I think she was with a group of other people - they were all wearing similar shirts."

Jennifer Katz inhaled sharply through her nose and pursed her lips. "It sounds like Dawn Thrasher."

We all turned at a crashing sound. Harry had been clearing a table nearby and dropped a tray of bottles and glasses. "Sorry!" he called, looking flustered.

"Who?" I asked, turning back to Jennifer Katz.

"Dawn Thrasher. She's kind of a professional troublemaker. She's a preservation activist. But I don't think that's the only item on her agenda."

"What do you mean?"

"I'm sorry, I really do need to get home."

And she was gone, disappearing around the corner of the building in a flurry of fluttering skirts that reminded me of Miss Nancy.

Petreski Barges In

MY BRAIN was still fried from the afternoon's exam, and I was supposed to be taking a nap, but was really lying on the sofa replaying the conversation I'd had with Tom Wilton that afternoon. He seemed like a nice enough guy, but he also seemed isolated and lonely, and I didn't want him latching on to me, which was the vibe I was getting. I did worry about Murphy, though, and was trying to figure out how I could get to see him without giving Tom the wrong idea.

I was drawing a complete blank and turning my thoughts to dinner when there was a knock at my door. "Nevermore," I whispered to myself, rolling to my feet. I was in a punchy mood and I didn't recognize the knock. "Who is it?" I called.

"Petreski! Open up!"

Cripes! The fuzz! "Just a sec!" I checked the mirror by the door and I looked decent – I hadn't changed when I got home so I was still wearing jeans and my shirt didn't stink. I grabbed a tin of mints from the basket on the bookshelf and popped a couple in my mouth, then took a deep breath and opened the door.

"Detective Petreski, what a surprise. Were you in the neighborhood?"

He looked me up and down before answering. "Are you alone?"

"Um, why?"

"I mean, do you have company? Am I interrupting? Do you have a minute?"

"For you, Detective Petreski, I have two." I stepped back and gestured for him to come inside.

He stepped past me, and I caught a whiff of musk and citrus and something herbal. He smelled as good as he looked, in that damn tailored suit and silk tie. I looked down at my bare toes and the ragged hem of my jeans, and felt underdressed in my own home. I sighed and tried to push past my weird mood.

"What?" Petreski turned to face me.

"Nothing," I shook my head. "Today has put me in a shitty mood."

He studied me for a minute, and for a second he looked kind of sympathetic. That was a nice thought.

"Did you need something?" I asked. Our weird breakfast from the day before had left me off balance, and I really needed to know where I stood with this man. My life was more complicated than I really felt equipped to deal with right now.

"We need to talk."

"About what?" I asked. I turned away from him and walked over to look out one of the front windows. The squirrel wasn't here at the moment, but it was only a matter of time. I heard Petreski moving around the apartment, but didn't turn to see what he was doing. As long as he didn't make a mess, I didn't care. It had been that kind of day. "I was at Ground Up this afternoon and Jennifer Katz came over to talk to me."

"You're popular all of a sudden."

"I'm charming and approachable."

"Hmm. What did Jennifer Katz want?"

"To apologize for her husband threatening me."

"Josh Katz threatened you? Why am I just now hearing about this?"

"Um, I've been busy and it slipped my mind?"

"Tell me."

I sighed and told him about my confrontation with Katz, his wife's apology, and her identification of the woman her husband had spoken to at the crime scene. All the while I could hear him rummaging around, but I knew he was listening.

"Is this… Jake, what is this doing in here?" He sounded pissed, so I turned to see what he was talking about.

He was standing in front of the refrigerator, the freezer door open and a baggie in his hand. I'd forgotten about that.

"It's medicinal."

"Jake…"

"Look, my spiritual advisor recommended it. Said it might help stop the crazy dreams."

"Did it?"

"No. It just made me sick. I think I might be allergic to it. So lame. Are you going to bust me for having it?"

He shook his head and tossed it back in the freezer. "I should, just to teach you a lesson. Maybe some other time."

He shifted his search to the 'fridge and found a beer that met his standards, then moved on to the only drawer to root around for a bottle opener.

"Make yourself at home, Detective Petreski, by all means."

The bottle open, he took a long pull from it before shifting his focus to me. It was more than a little disconcerting.

"Should you be drinking on duty?"

"Not on duty."

"Oh. So, then to what do I owe the honor?" I leaned against the window frame, crossing my arms across my chest and trying to look all badass and unperturbed. Yeah, right.

"The honor?"

"Of your company?"

He didn't answer. After another big swig of beer he started walking the perimeter of my apartment, flipped the light on and off in the bathroom, and was heading for the closet when I cleared my throat.

"If you're not on duty, you don't get to look in my closet."

He turned back to me and shrugged.

"Seriously, Petreski, what are you doing here?"

"Curiosity."

"That's it? Curiosity?"

"You're a curious guy, Jake Hillebrand."

"I am?"

"For instance, I know you're twenty-six, but you've been a full time student for years, have no student loans, and still haven't graduated. You've got a trust fund, but you live in a one room studio. Your father owns a whole string of car dealerships, but you drive a four-year-old hatchback that looks like it's been in a demolition derby."

"Not that it's any of your business, but I haven't been able to decide on a major. I can afford to pay my tuition and I don't want debt. Yeah, I have a trust fund, but it's not huge. It's from my grandmother and it's enough to cover tuition and living expenses and a little extra. It's enough to live on, but not extravagantly. And yeah, my dad owns car dealerships, but have you seen how I drive? My dad will only fix me up with a new one every five years, so I've got to make this one last."

"And the apartment?"

"I love this place. It has charm."

"It is nice. But what'll you do if the owners decide to sell? Places like this are getting razed for McMansions all the time."

"They won't."

"How can you be so sure?"

"My parents own it. If they ever want to sell, they have to give my trust first refusal. I'm not going anywhere, and neither is this building."

Petreski started another circuit of the room, stopping at the bookshelf by the door and picking up the catnip mouse I'd swiped from Don's stash, in case Boo got bored. "You have a cat?" he asked, sniffing the mouse.

"Not exactly."

He continued his prowl, now looking out the first of the windows on the front of the building. "Nice trees."

"Yeah."

He moved to the second window and looked up into the higher branches. "What's up with that squirrel?"

I rolled my eyes. "Just ignore him. He's a weirdo."

He was standing in front of the third window now, the one I was standing by, and still looking up at the squirrel. "I don't like the way he's looking at me."

"He's very territorial. He probably sees you as a threat."

"Probably." He took another swig of the beer. It was almost gone now and I couldn't remember whether I had another one. "Do you?"

"Do I what?"

"See me as a threat?"

"Are you planning to arrest me?"

"No."

"Then why should I see you as a threat?"

Petreski sighed and polished off the beer, setting the empty bottle on the windowsill. "You really have no sense of self-preservation, do you?" he asked, turning to look at me.

"I do. Just because I don't see you as a threat doesn't mean I have no sense of caution."

"Really? Because you let me in."

"But I know you. And you're a cop, right? Trying to solve Wilton's murder? Why should I be afraid?"

He leaned his forearm against the window sash and looked down at me like he was genuinely concerned for my safety.

"Predators come in all shapes and sizes, Jake. You need to be careful. Don't trust anyone until we've found out who killed Wilton. They may think you know something and you could be in danger."

I rolled my eyes and he reached out to grab my chin and turn me back to face him.

"I'm serious, here. This is not a joke and don't roll your eyes over this. Promise me you'll be careful."

He looked deadly serious, and for a second I was a little afraid. Not of him, but of the power he had and what he could do if he had to. I nodded, and his gaze dropped. I had had my suspicions, but it was still a surprise when his lips came down on mine.

I could smell the beer he'd been drinking, and his heavy stubble was an unfamiliar roughness on the edge of my lip. I had barely recovered myself enough to start kissing back when he pulled away.

"Wha– I thought I was a suspect?"

He shifted his hand from my chin to my throat, holding me in place while his thumb stroked up and down.

"No. We cleared you, much to Detective Perez's chagrin."

"And when were you planning to tell me this?"

"I just did." He released me, picked up his beer bottle, and headed for the kitchen.

"Wh… where are you going?" I wasn't finished with the kissing, to be perfectly honest.

"You got any more beer?"

"I don't know. What are you doing?" He was back in the freezer, pulling out the baggie.

"Getting rid of this evidence."

"I told you, I'm not going to smoke it."

"Yeah, so I don't want it around here where someone else could find it and you could get in trouble."

"Oh. Yeah, that makes sense." Wow, that was really thoughtful. And then he dug through the drawer again before turning on one of the stove burners and lighting up that damn joint. He wasn't thoughtful at all. He just wanted to smoke my pot.

"Close your mouth and open a window, Jake," he said around the joint hanging out of one side of his mouth as he took off his suit jacket and loosened his tie. I was in too much shock to complain, and just did as I was told for once.

"You want a beer?" he asked, and I nodded. The squirrel had hopped down to the windowsill when I opened the window, so I went to the kitchen for some sunflower seeds.

It was a tight fit in the kitchen with Petreski in there, but I squeezed past him to get to the cabinet with the seeds.

"Are you feeding that thing?"

"Yes. And no, he won't come inside, and no, he does not have rabies."

"Geez, kid. You're gonna name him next."

I thought about it for a second. "His name is Raymond."

"You named him Raymond?"

I thought about it again. "No. I didn't name him, that's just his... oh... Oh, shit. How do I *know* his name is Raymond? How do I know that?" I turned to Petreski, who was standing there staring at me with that damn joint hanging from the corner of his mouth. I turned to the squirrel who was sitting on the windowsill watching me. "How do I know your name is Raymond? And what the hell kind of name is Raymond for a squirrel, anyway?"

Raymond let out a high pitched squeak and flicked his tail.

"Sorry. I didn't know squirrels had names. Oh, shit. I need to sit down." I had just offended a squirrel and I actually felt kind of bad about it.

Petreski walked me over to the sofa, one hand under my arm holding me up, the other hand carrying an opened beer. "Raymond's seeds," I said, trying to focus on something normal.

"What?"

"In the kitchen. Sunflower seeds for Raymond. The window is open. He has expectations and I can't let him down."

"Fine. I'll find them. Drink this." He pressed the beer into my hand and I heard him rattling around in my tiny kitchen. He came out a minute later with a handful of seeds and put them on the windowsill. Raymond chattered a little, but didn't fuss too much at having a stranger so close. "You feeling any better?" He asked, coming to sit beside me. I nodded and he took a drag off his – my – joint and tamped the ashes into his empty beer bottle.

We sat there for a few minutes, me drinking, him smoking, Raymond chomping his way through his seeds.

"You had an a-ha moment."

I nodded.

"This is some good shit." He took another hit. "You got any more?"

I shook my head.

"Eh, probably just as well."

We sat for another few minutes, drinking, smoking, and eating. Raymond finished his seeds and disappeared into the tree. Petreski polished off the joint and dropped the butt into the bottle before setting it on the floor. I gulped down the last of my beer and Petreski took the bottle from me.

"So… you and animals."

"What?"

He shrugged. "You tell me."

I went to stand by the open window to get some fresh air. Just the smell of the smoke was making me feel queasy. "I don't know. I've always liked animals, and animals always seemed to like me well enough."

"You ever have any pets when you were a kid?"

I shook my head. "No. Whenever we would go visit a friend or relative who had a pet, I'd get too excited playing with them. I'd get – overstimulated my mother would call it. She said no pets. So, no."

"Maybe if you'd had pets when you were young – been around animals more – this wouldn't be such a shock now."

"Maybe, but why now? Why not before? I see people walking by with their dogs all the time. I see cats on the street. There's animals all over the place, so why now?"

"You've never had a pet?"

"No, I told you."

"You've never taken care of an animal or formed any kind of bond with one?"

"No."

"Until now."

"What? No."

He looked at me like I was stupid, and I turned to look out the open window. I couldn't see much, since the sun was pretty much down by now. I could sense Raymond somewhere up in the branches of the tree where he probably had a cozy nest. "Furry little asshole. It's all his fault."

"He didn't do anything. You opened the window – literally and figuratively. You forged the bond and, for some reason, because of some dormant aptitude or ability, you got more than you bargained for."

"Oh, man." I flopped back down on the sofa, wishing I had another beer or six. "What do I do now? I can't traipse around Houston like some deranged Doctor Doolittle, talking to animals."

"You could be a charming eccentric. This neighborhood needs more of them these days."

"Jerk. I'm too young, and I don't have enough money to be eccentric." I thought about my best friend planning to leash-train his three-legged cat. The neighborhood would probably be fine, eccentric-wise.

"You're probably right."

He leaned back, and we both stared up at the ceiling.

"I wish I had another beer," I said.

"I wish you had another joint."

"I don't. Do I have more beer?"

"Yes. Do you have any food?"

"No. There's a menu on the 'fridge. Order a pizza, but you're paying."

"Why do I have to pay? You're the one with the trust fund."

"You smoked all my pot. You made me have a fricking epiphany. You pay for the pizza."

"Fine. Epiphany? Who uses words like epiphany these days?"

"People who read books."

I could hear him in the kitchen calling for pizza delivery. He ordered my favorite, probably guessing that was the best bet since I had hi-lighted it on the menu. Maybe he was a tiny bit thoughtful.

He came back a few minutes later with two open beers and sat down next to me – a little closer this time – before handing me one. I still wasn't sure what he was up to.

"What are you up to?"

"What do you mean? Who says I'm up to anything?"

"Why are you here? Did you come over here to mess with my head, try to get me to admit I'm some kind of animal psychic or something?"

"Not exactly. Although that was a bonus."

"Me having a meltdown? You enjoyed that?"

"I'd hardly call it a meltdown."

"Whatever it was, I didn't particularly enjoy it."

"Sorry."

"So?"

He shrugged and I watched him drink beer for a few seconds before facing forward and taking a sip of my own.

"I was curious."

"You said that before. Curious about what?"

"About you. About how you would act. And we've cleared you, but not Don."

"What the fuck?"

"Hold on, hold on." He reached over to pat my hand where it was resting on my thigh. Without thinking I flipped my hand over and he slid his fingers between mine. "I know he didn't do it, but we haven't been able to confirm his alibi."

"How were you so sure I really was a – whatever I am? What am I, anyway?"

"I don't know. Maybe you should ask your spiritual advisor."

He giggled, and I knew it was probably because he had just inhaled that joint, but no one giggles at Miss Nancy!

"Sorry. Sorry," he said. I must have looked pretty pissed off. "Gut instinct."

"Gut instinct? Cops really put stock in that?"

"I do." He was dead serious now, and I wondered what had happened. He was still holding my hand. He had nice hands – I thought they were nice, anyway. They were exceptionally well groomed, and I wondered whether he had his nails professionally manicured. There were little dark hairs poking out from under his sleeve and a few sprouted from the backs of his fingers. He really was very hairy, and I worried about the state of my drains in the event he ever – and I knew I was jumping the gun here – but in the event he ever had call to shower at my apartment.

"What?" He asked.

"Nothing." I took another sip of beer so I wouldn't have to look at him.

"Jake." I recognized that tone, and turned to meet his gaze. It was time for *that* part of the conversation, and I wasn't sure I was ready for it. I took another, bigger, sip of beer.

"Why did you kiss me?" I guess my mouth was ready – it was just my brain that hadn't caught up.

"Did you not want me to kiss you?"

"I didn't say that. But I wasn't sure you even, well, liked me. So why kiss me?"

Right then the downstairs buzzer went off and he let go of my hand. "Saved by the bell," I heard him mutter as he got up to go get the pizza. I guess he preferred to be the one asking the questions.

I drank more beer and waited. He was back in a few minutes with the box, and that was when I realized he wasn't wearing his shoulder holster. "Where's your gun?"

"What?"

"Your gun – aren't you supposed to be, like, armed or something?"

"Told you – I'm off duty. Why? Worried about me?" He grinned and put the pizza box on the coffee table. I went to the kitchen to get plates and napkins and check the status of my beer supply.

"No."

"Liar. If it makes you feel any better, I've got a back-up in an ankle holster. God, you ask a lot of questions."

"Yeah. So answer some. Why are you really here, and why did you kiss me?"

"I'm here because… because I needed to make sure you're safe. And I kissed you because I couldn't *not* kiss you."

"That makes no sense."

He shrugged and looked away. "That's what Perez said."

"You talked to Perez about me? About… about me like that?" I wasn't sure how I felt about that. Exposed – especially since it was Perez and I was convinced *she* didn't like me. But he wouldn't talk to her about me if he wasn't interested in me, right? "I *know* she doesn't like me."

"It's not that she doesn't like you. She just sees that, well, she sees that you have the potential to be a big distraction for me, and she's very protective."

I liked the idea of being a distraction, but not if it put him in any danger.

"Maybe you're the one who needs to be careful," I told him.

"Maybe. And maybe we could just eat this pizza, have another beer, and then I could kiss you goodnight and go home. I'd really like to give that a try."

"You mean, like a date? Detective Petreski, did you come over here for an ambush date?"

He rubbed the back of his neck and looked up at me. "Maybe? How's that working out, by the way?"

I tried to look stern, but I was already thinking about the goodnight kiss, and liking the sound of that. "I'm not going to call you Detective Petreski."

"Ruben."

"Huh?"

"Ruben. It's my name."

"Okay, Ruben. We'll eat this pizza, and drink these beers. We'll even do the goodnight kiss thing. But you don't get to boss me around. Also, try to convince Detective Perez to stop giving me the evil eye. She's starting to give me a complex."

"I can't make any guarantees about Perez, but I promise I'll try."

"Fair enough." I moved to sit next to him on the sofa and he opened the pizza box.

We had a conversation – a real conversation, not an interrogation. We talked about books and movies and my studies. I told him about Miss Nancy – although not that she was the actual source of the joint. We talked about places we had been, places we wanted to go, favorite restaurants, and before I knew it, it had taken us three hours to eat a pizza and he needed to leave.

He put his coat back on as we walked to the door, and he stood there with his hand on the doorknob, looking down at me, and for the first time he didn't look sure of himself.

"Look," he said, "if you don't want -"

I cut him off, grabbing the lapels of his jacket and leaning in to shut him up with a kiss. He had better reflexes than I did, I guess, because he was kissing me back right away. It was better than the first one, because this time I got to really pay attention and appreciate it. His lips were warm and firm, and I could feel the strength in his arms when he wrapped them around me, one at my waist and the other at my upper back.

I felt the scrape of his stubble as he adjusted the angle, and I released his lapels to slide my hands up and wrap my arms around his neck. He was only a couple of inches taller than me, but I loved the size and the strength of him. He felt solid and real, more real than anyone else I had ever kissed. It frightened me a little, but not enough to make me want to stop.

"Jake," he said, pulling back after a few minutes.

"Hmm?"

"Jake, look at me."

I opened my eyes. He sounded serious.

"Promise me you'll be careful."

I nodded.

"Don't take any chances. I'm serious."

"I promise."

"When this case is done, we'll go out. On a real date. If you want?"

I nodded again. "You're probably not supposed to be doing this, are you?"

"No. The timing sucks, but like I said before, I couldn't not."

"I don't understand."

"I'll tell you when we go on that real date." He kissed me on the forehead, and then he was gone, slipping out the door and down the stairs. The door across the landing opened and Don stuck his head out.

"Was that Detective Petreski?" he asked.

"Yep."

"Are you in trouble?"

"Hmm. Not sure."

"Geez. What did he want?"

Now that was a loaded question. "To let me know he's not straight."

Don rolled his eyes. "Great. Try not to get your heart broken."

I shook my head. I don't know how I knew, but it was the same feeling of certainty I'd had about so many other things lately. "I won't. Oh, the squirrel's name is Raymond, by the way."

"Shit. You named it?"

"No. That's just his name. He told me."

"Who? Petreski?"

"No. Raymond. How would Petreski know Raymond's name?"

"I'm too tired for this conversation. I'll see you tomorrow."

He disappeared back into his apartment, and I tidied away the dishes and bottles from dinner. I was getting ready to take a shower before going to bed when I heard a familiar scratching sound. Sure enough, there was a black paw curled under the door.

"Boo," I said, opening the door for him to slip in. "I'm supposed to be careful, but I guess it's okay to let *you* in."

Boo made his usual regal circuit of the room, tail held high. I left him to it and went into the bathroom to take a shower and brush my teeth. At one point Boo stuck his head into the shower. I flicked some water at him and he ducked back. "Don't be a perv, Boo!" I told him.

I pushed the shower curtain back and started drying off, Boo observing from the dry safety of the doorway. "It's okay, Boo. No more splashing."

He meowed at me, and I felt chastised. "Sorry, Boo." The big black cat came into the room and jumped into the tub, where he started licking at the water clinging to the sides. I finished drying off, brushed my teeth, and pulled on a pair of boxer shorts.

"Ready for bed, Boo?" I called as I pulled the covers back on the bed. I made sure a window was open enough for Boo to leave when he wanted, then climbed into bed. Boo came trotting in from the bathroom, jumped up on the bed, and tromped around for a while before curling up next to me. I stroked his silky fur and he started to purr.

"You have a big day, Boo?" I asked. He rolled over, exposing his belly, and I stroked it. "Yeah, me too. You're not my first visitor of the evening, you know."

Boo rolled again and came to head-butt my chin. "Aww, don't be jealous, Boo." I laughed when he started licking me with his rough, pink tongue.

"Okay, okay. Enough of that. Yeah. Second-best kiss I've had all day." I kissed the top of Boo's head, and he settled down, stretching out on the bed and purring loudly as we both drifted off to sleep.

I dreamed that night, but they weren't the disturbing dreams like I'd been having. This time I dreamed about Petreski – Ruben. It was steamy and felt so real that I was surprised when I woke up to find myself alone in my bed. Except for Boo, of course, who was watching me with that smug face cats get sometimes. "Go to sleep, Boo," I said, rolling over and punching my pillow. "Go to sleep."

Can't a Guy Just Get a Cup of Coffee?

OH, BLESSED Saturday, I thought to myself when I woke up the next morning and realized I didn't have to get out of bed. I grabbed a book off my bedside table and then tossed it aside when I realized it was a school book. I had better luck with the next one. Uh-oh. Paranormal romance – better not let Don catch me reading this. I bunched my pillows up and settled in for some light reading.

I must have dozed off again, because a knocking at my door woke me. My first thought was that maybe Petreski had come back, but that was just wishful thinking. He was probably out hunting down murderers or eating donuts or whatever hunky police detectives did on the weekend. Probably not donuts, if he was going to keep his figure.

Another knock broke my train of thought, and Don's voice carried through the door. "Jake? You up?"

"Almost. Hang on." I pushed the covers aside and staggered to the door. I could see one of Bridger's tiny paws flailing around through the crack below the door. It must be a cat thing. I bent to bat at the paw with my finger before opening the door to let my annoying neighbors in.

"Planning to sleep the day away?" Don asked as he came in and Bridger made a dash for the sofa.

"If you're going to wake me up on a Saturday, at least make yourself useful and start the coffee. And don't let your cat claw up my sofa."

By the time I came out of the bathroom refreshed and dressed the coffee was almost ready and Don was on the sofa distracting Bridger from the upholstery.

"So what's up?" I asked as I went over to make my bed. Don accuses me of being a neat freak, but when you live in a one room studio it can start looking dumpy fast – you gotta stay on top of that, you know?

"Was I imagining things last night, or did Detective Petreski come over here, and did you tell me you named that squirrel Raymond?"

"You're a little off, but yes, Petreski was here. And I didn't name the squirrel, that's just his name. It's… kind of hard to explain."

Don got up to pour our coffee. "Give it a shot."

I sighed as I sat down and took a sip. "Okay, yeah. Petreski showed up last night. He kind of poked around the apartment a bit, found the joint I had stashed in the freezer –"

"Wait, what? Since when do you stash joints in your freezer?"

"It's not like that. Miss Nancy said it might help stop the dreams, so she gave me a couple. I tried one, but it made me sick. I was going to give the other one back to her, but Petreski found it before I could."

"Oh, crap. What did he do?"

"Smoked it."

"What?!"

"Yeah. He said he was getting rid of the evidence, but I think the good detective is just as human as the rest of us."

"So, not a werewolf, then?" Don asked with a smirk.

"Ha ha. No, not a werewolf."

"Okay, then what?"

"Um, things are kind of getting out of order, but he kind of forced me into admitting that I have some sort of weird psychic connection with animals. Some animals."

"I told you so."

"That is so unattractive."

Don shrugged. "So what's this about the squirrel, then?"

I told him about how I'd just suddenly *known* the squirrel's name, how I could tell I'd insulted the squirrel, and Detective Petreski's theory about how and why I'd suddenly started experiencing this strange animal connection.

"What do you think of this theory of his?" Don asked when I'd finished.

"I don't know. But I'm going to run it by Miss Nancy. I guess it makes sense, in a way."

"So what did you mean when you said he came over to let you know he wasn't straight?"

"A gentleman doesn't kiss and tell," I said, sipping my coffee. I was trying for prim, but I probably came across as smug.

"Are you… Did you? You and Petreski?"

"Whatever you're thinking, stop. Aside from inviting himself over, and snooping around my apartment and smoking my pot and drinking my beer, he was a perfect gentleman. Practically. There was no…" I waved my hand around.

"What does," Don waved his hand around, "mean?"

"You know. Stuff. Sex stuff. I said *kiss* and tell."

"You realize you just told me, right?"

"Please don't mess with my head this morning. Be a dear and pour me another cup of coffee, would you?" I batted my eyelashes. Don rolled his eyes, but he did pour me another cup.

"So what are you going to do today? Study? More midterms?"

"No. I have a paper due right after spring break, but it's practically done."

Don muttered something that sounded like "OCD" but I ignored him.

"Did you have something in mind?"

"Not really," Don answered. "I'm working tonight. You?"

"I was thinking about heading over to Ground Up and seeing who decides to unload on me today."

"Seriously?"

"Kind of. Do I have one of those faces?"

"Maybe. You sure do seem to be attracting a lot of trouble lately."

"Bleh. Oh, and I need to call my parents later. They want me to come visit. They'll probably invite you, too, you know." My parents love Don. They think he's a good influence.

"Maybe I'll go. When were you thinking of going?"

"Spring break is week after next. I figured I'd go for a couple of days then."

"I thought students were supposed to go to the beach and get drunk for spring break."

"I'm a grown-up. I can get drunk anytime I want, which is never because I hate feeling out of control and then sick the next day. Besides, most of my college buddies have graduated already. Oh, crap."

"What?"

"I just realized something. I think I might be a nerd."

"There's no shame in being a nerd."

"I know that. It's just that I'm just now realizing it. Even when I was a kid I was kind of an uptight bookworm. I never even went through a rebellious phase."

"Yeah, you sound pretty boring. You know, for an animal psychic who finds dead bodies and talks to squirrels. Named Raymond, of all things."

"Don't make fun of his name, dude. I think he's sensitive about it."

Don rolled his eyes. "Whatever. Let's go to Ground Up, have a sandwich, maybe a beer – because I think you need to incorporate more day drinking into your routine – and see what happens."

I put some sunflower seeds on the windowsill for Raymond while Don went back to his place for the cat sling, and the three of us headed off to Ground Up. God help us.

❧

I was at a seat by the window, and I was looking towards the counter when it happened or I never would have seen it. Harry had just finished serving a customer when the bell rang and he turned towards the door. I'd never actually seen anyone go white as a ghost before, but Harry did, right before his eyes bugged out. When I turned to see what he was looking at, my eyes probably bugged out, too.

Standing in the doorway was the blond woman I had seen speak to Josh Katz at the crime scene. From the way she was looking at Harry, these two had to know each other, and this was not a happy reunion.

They looked at each other for a few moments before she went up to the counter and ordered. Harry served her, but he didn't make chit-chat with her like he would with any other customer.

"Don," I said, keeping my voice low even though there was music playing and we were out of earshot of the counter, "it's that Dawn Thrasher lady."

"Who?" Don turned to look and I kicked him under the table.

"Don't look! Dawn Thrasher. The one Josh Katz was talking to and Jennifer Katz didn't want to talk about."

"Oh."

"I think she and Harry must know each other, because when she came in he looked really shocked, and she looked kind of confused and pissed off when she saw him. Shh! She's heading this way!"

"I wasn't saying anything." Don looked at me like I was a spaz, which maybe I was – at the moment. I think this whole dreams and murder thing was starting to make me paranoid.

She didn't say anything to us, and sat down at the next table, back to the wall. She took out a laptop – not a sleek Apple like most of the other patrons, but something older and heavier. It looked beat up, like maybe it had gotten knocked around as she traveled from hot spot to hot spot, stirring up trouble and leaving the locals to deal with the fallout.

I stared into my coffee mug, because in spite of Don's opinion that I needed a beer, I was still waking up and I needed caffeine. Don was keeping busy with a sandwich and some kind of healthy-looking seaweed salad thing. I had a sandwich, too, but I hadn't unwrapped it yet. After a few minutes of silence I realized someone was speaking to me.

"Huh? What? Sorry?" I looked up to see Dawn Thrasher looking at me.

"You were at the crime scene the other day. I'm right, yeah? When Clarence – Clarence Wilton was found?"

"Y – yes. We were. But I'm not supposed to talk about it, I don't think."

She waved her hand. Obviously such restrictions were for other people, not her. "You found him, right?"

I traded a look with Don. He didn't say anything, just kept eating. I could see I was on my own here.

"I'm not supposed to –"

"Of course you did. That's why you were *inside* the police tape, not outside with the rest of us. And you had his dog. Why did you have his dog? Did you find it?" She was asking questions, but it didn't feel like she was asking me so much as just speculating out loud, so I didn't say anything.

She looked from me to Don, then back again. "Yeah. That must be it."

"I'm not… I can't…"

"Oh, don't worry. I'm not going to get you boys in trouble. It seems you've ruffled up Josh's feathers, though, so you might want to be careful there. Word to the wise, you know."

"Josh Katz?" Don asked.

"Yes, that's the one. Such a jumpy man. Very… what's the word… volatile?"

I nodded, agreeing with that much.

"Yes, volatile. The kind of passion that can accomplish great things if properly channeled, but on an interpersonal level… Well, it's not so nice to be around every day, if you get my meaning."

I didn't say anything, and returned her gaze. I wasn't entirely sure I understood her, but I felt uneasy and was starting to consider heading off to Austin today and staying with my folks until this whole thing was over with.

She turned back to her computer and started typing. She must have said what she had to say, and I was ready to go home. "You done?" I asked Don.

He nodded and gathered up his trash. We started walking home, me carrying my still unopened sandwich.

"That was weird," Don said after we had crossed the street.

"Yeah. So, she and Harry know each other, I'm sure of it."

"And she knows Katz."

"I think – I'm just guessing – but I think she knew Clarence Wilton, too."

"What makes you say that?"

"She called him Clarence before she corrected herself – did you catch that?"

"No, not really."

"And she recognized his dog."

"Maybe she saw you hand the dog over to his family."

"Maybe, but it feels weird."

"Yeah."

"And why make it a point to talk to us? Was she threatening us? Telling us that stuff about Katz?"

"She could be an over-sharer."

I thought about that for a minute. "No, I don't think so. I think everything Dawn Thrasher says is very well thought out. She doesn't strike me as the kind of person who has unnecessary conversations or shares unnecessary details. She only lets other people see what she wants them to see. Usually."

"Usually?"

"When she walked into Ground Up she was genuinely shocked to see Harry. It took her a minute to look cool and collected again."

We walked on in silence for a couple of minutes.

"We should tell Detective Petreski about this," Don said.

"Yeah. You call him and we'll do it on speaker. When we get home."

"You don't want to talk to him?"

"Of course I do. But I want it all above-board. I don't think he's supposed to be fraternizing or whatever. I don't want him to get in trouble. And I don't want to get in trouble for not telling him something we should tell him."

"Okay. We'll do it your way."

We called Petreski, and told him everything Dawn Thrasher had said. I told him about the strange reactions when Harry and Dawn had seen each other. I could hear Petreski sigh over the phone.

"Jake…"

"What?" I knew he was going to chew me out. Gently, but still, I didn't have to like it.

"I told you to be careful. You promised."

"What wasn't careful? I wasn't alone – Don was with me. We were in a public place and all that happened was that a woman I don't know talked to me. In broad daylight."

"You're attracting too much attention. I don't like this."

"I can't help it if everyone goes there – it's the only coffee shop in walking distance. I can't just shut myself up in my apartment all day every day. I have to go to school and the grocery store and do laundry and stuff."

I could hear him sigh again. I knew he was worried about me, but I wasn't going to change my whole routine. I had a life to live.

"If you could just lay low for a few days…"

"But –"

"Okay, look. If you'll just do your best to avoid Dawn Thrasher and the Katzes. Can you do that?"

"Why? Why them in particular?"

"Jake, please."

"I'll talk to him," said Don, the traitor.

We ended the call.

"He really does sound concerned."

"Yeah, I guess," I said.

"I thought you'd be happy about that."

"Sure, but I don't like being ordered around. And I'm not a helpless kid. I can take care of myself. And it's not like anything's going to happen to me in a coffee shop or a laundromat."

"That's probably what Clarence Wilton thought."

That put things right back into perspective.

"And if Detective Petreski's worried about you, he can't concentrate on his job, and that could be dangerous for him."

Man, Don could fight dirty when he wanted to. "Okay, I get it. I know I need to be careful. But I've got to do laundry. It's a borderline emergency at this point."

"Can it wait until tomorrow? I'll go with you. And you can come to work with me tonight. You can sit at the end of the bar and drink ginger ale all night, but at least you won't be here alone."

"We can do the laundry tomorrow, but I'm staying here. I'll lock the door, and I won't let anyone in, cross my heart."

"Fine. I'll text Detective Petreski that he can stop worrying. He should give you his phone number, you know."

"No. Not until the case is finished."

"Sometimes I really don't get you."

"Yeah, well, I just want to keep things as simple as possible for now. And other than him coming over last night, everything has been completely above-board. I want to keep it that way."

"I guess I'm just surprised that someone who hasn't been able to choose a major after seven years and visits a spiritual advisor and was trying to convince me he was a werewolf just a few days ago can be so together and mature at the same time."

I shrugged. I could feel the sting of truth in his words. "Just text him, okay? Tell him I'll be careful and won't go out unnecessarily, but I'm still going to classes."

"Okay, okay."

❧

I was a good boy the rest of the day. Don went with me to the grocery store and brought Bridger and his things over to my place before leaving for work. I stayed inside the rest of the afternoon and evening.

I didn't really mind. I had studying to do, and Raymond came to visit. I put some sunflower seeds on the windowsill and crouched down to watch Raymond eat. Bridger was curious, but stayed on the sofa. He wasn't that much bigger than Raymond, and I don't think he knew what to make of the squirrel.

"So, Raymond," I said, keeping my voice soft. "We haven't really had a chance to talk since, well, you know. Last night."

Raymond cocked his head, but didn't stop nibbling at the seed in his paws.

"I don't know how much you understand of what I'm saying."

Bits of hull flew as Raymond chewed on.

"I am sorry about what I said about your name. It's a perfectly nice name, I just didn't realize it was popular in the, um, squirrel community. Anyway," I cleared my throat. "Anyway, I hope we can be friends and keep getting along."

Raymond finished the last of the seeds and lowered his front paws to the windowsill. He looked at me, nose twitching.

"Does that mean yes?"

His nose twitched again, and he was gone into the tree. He hadn't chattered or scolded me, so I guessed we were okay.

I closed the window – I didn't know how far Bridger's curiosity would take him, and how far he could go, even with only three legs. Best not to take chances.

Bridger explored and played and chased toys around the apartment while I tried to study. I wasn't accomplishing much, so after a while I set my laptop up on the coffee table and stretched out on the sofa to binge watch some TV. Nothing with murders in it, though.

I had just finished washing my dinner dishes, feeling very virtuous because I had cooked myself an actual healthy meal thanks to the day's grocery run, when I heard the scratching at the door.

"Sounds like company's come, Bridger." I said, checking for the paw under the door to make sure it really was Boo and not a murderous neighbor. Bridger perked up his ears and started moving towards the door.

"Hey, Boo!" I said, opening the door. "Ooh! Who's your friend?" Sitting a couple of feet behind Boo was an elegant cat with wavy calico fur – I'd never seen a Rex in real life before and thought maybe they were pretty rare. Boo came inside, and when the other cat didn't move he turned and meowed at it. "Come on inside," I encouraged it. "The more the merrier!" The cat gave me an uncertain look, then trotted after Boo.

"I have to warn you, Boo. I'm babysitting tonight so you'll have to put up with Bridger again." Boo had already made a beeline for the sofa and he and Bridger were sniffing at each other. The new cat approached slowly, and sniffed at the young one.

While the cats introduced themselves I fixed a bigger bowl of water and opened the window.

"So, is this your girlfriend, Boo?" I asked, after watching the two grown cats fuss over the little one. The new cat looked up at me with golden eyes, but quickly turned her attention back to Bridger.

Boo left the other two cats to join me on the sofa, curling up on my lap and purring like a motorboat. I guess house arrest was okay as long as I had a friend like Boo to cuddle up with.

"So what do you do all day, huh Boo? You have someone else you hang out with during the day? Am I your dirty little secret?" I giggled, and Boo batted at my hand with a paw.

I felt the sofa dip and turned to see that the lady cat had jumped up on the other end and was sniffing around. I held my hand out towards her and wiggled my fingers. "Hey, kitty," I called softly. She turned to look at me, saw my fingers, and hissed – not loud, just enough to let me know she wasn't interested.

Boo growled, also not loud, and the female cowered. It was obvious who was in charge here. "It's okay, Boo." I gave him a little squeeze and he relaxed. "We just need to get to know each other better."

It was strange, though. I'd never been hissed at by a cat before, or growled at, either. Animals tended to like me.

I watched the lady cat sniff around a bit more, and held still as she approached me. She sniffed my arm, never taking her eyes off my face. When she placed a tentative paw on my leg, I felt Boo stiffen and start to rumble. She drew back, and jumped down to the floor to play with Bridger.

"Now, Boo," I scolded, "there's no need to be territorial."

The lady cat didn't stay much longer, and left by way of the open window. Bridger watched her leave, and followed her as far as the floor beneath the windowsill. I could see him wiggling his little butt like he was going to try to jump up to the windowsill, but before I could move to stop him, Boo had leaped from my lap and intercepted the kitten before he could jump. Picking Bridger up by the scruff of his neck, Boo brought him back to the sofa and deposited him in my lap. Bridger protested a bit in his tiny kitten voice, but didn't get any sympathy.

"Wow, Boo." That was all I could think to say. It was kind of freaky, how Boo knew what to do and did it. "You're something else, Boo. You're gonna be a good kitty-daddy someday."

I restarted my laptop and settled in to watch, this time with two cats on my lap.

Can't a Guy Just Do His Laundry?

ON SUNDAY, Don and I loaded our laundry into the back of my car and drove to the laundromat. I separated my laundry into three washers (like I said, it was a near emergency) and settled down in a chair to watch the traffic go by. Don got waylaid by a couple of little old ladies who wanted to see what was in the cat sling, so I was sitting on my own when Harry came in.

He did a quick scan of the room, nodding at me before heading to a washer. I moved my backpack when he came over so he could sit.

"Hey," he said.

"Hey. How's it going?"

"Not so good, actually."

I hadn't expected an honest answer. "Oh, sorry."

He shrugged. "It's… weird."

"Yeah. Weird pretty much describes my life lately."

"You remember the other day – when I told you about that girl I knew in college?"

"Yeah."

"I saw her the other day. She walked into my shop. How's *that* for weird? I mean, right after the police came, and we talked about her. She just shows up."

I had suspected as much, but I didn't say anything. As far as I was concerned, psychic dreams were weird. Seeing an old flame after talking about her was just coincidence.

"It seems like bad things always happen when she's around."

That got my attention. "What do you mean?"

"She was a firebrand. Ruthless. It was like… like she had no moral compass and no filter. She would do whatever it took. Say whatever she had to say. She used people – especially men." He stopped, staring off into the middle distance.

"What do you mean?"

"Like I said, we were toxic together. After I broke up with her, it wasn't two weeks before she had a new guy, and he was caught breaking into the same lab she'd wanted me to get into. She wanted good things, good changes, but she didn't always go about things the right way."

"I was there. When she came in? I saw her. She came over and talked to me. She had recognized me from the crime scene."

"Somehow that doesn't surprise me."

"That she talked to me?"

"That she was there. The controversy and the demonstrations around Wilton and his developments – that would be like catnip for Dawn."

"She didn't strike me as lacking a filter, though. The things she said to me – and Don – were quite pointed."

"She probably had to develop one to stay out of trouble. Whatever you do, don't rise to her bait, and don't let her get in your head. In fact, I'd recommend avoiding her as much as you can. That's what I'm planning to do."

I was getting tired of being told to avoid people, but in this case I had no problem going along with it. This sounded more like friendly advice than an order.

❧

Later, when I told Don about my conversation with Harry, he called Petreski and made me repeat the conversation for him. "He's going to get tired of us calling him," I sighed as we ended that call.

"He's going to get tired of you running around talking to people, more likely."

"I was at the laundromat minding my own business! I can't help it if people talk to me. I can't just run and hide whenever someone talks to me, can I?"

"Petreski would probably say you could."

"He's going to decide I'm too much trouble."

"Then try staying out of trouble."

"Dude. You are the one who got me into this! It was your idea to go check the bayou!"

Don was silent, and I realized I'd gone too far.

"Don, I –"

"Seriously? My fault?"

"I'm sorry, I –"

"Jesus, Jake. I've been nothing but supportive of you this entire time. All this crazy shit going on around you, and I never once batted an eye."

I hung my head. What could I say? He was right. "Don, I really –"

"Not right now, Jake. Just… not now, okay?"

Don left to go back to his apartment, and I started putting away my clean laundry. My towels and shirts and underwear were all folded the same in orderly stacks and I realized I probably was OCD. One more thing for Don to be right about.

I hated arguing with Don – he was my best friend and had been since we were fifteen, when he was the new nerdy kid and I was the noisy drama geek everyone was tired of telling to shut up. I'd never known when to keep quiet, had I? I wanted more than anything to go across the hall and apologize, but I let Don have his space. He knew I was sorry, and he'd be over soon to let me grovel properly.

Jake and Don Get Nosy

MONDAY MORNING, and it was hard to believe it had only been a week since we'd found Bridger and life had started getting seriously weird. I had to go to class today, and I needed to figure out a way to avoid Tom Wilton.

I got to campus around my usual time, and waited in my car for a few minutes, looking around to make sure I didn't see Tom anywhere before getting out and walking straight to the building where class was held. I felt ridiculous, slipping into the room at the last minute and not looking around before heading straight to my seat and getting ready for class. So far, so good. I just needed to repeat the procedure on the way out. For all I knew, Tom might not even be here today – I had been too afraid of making eye contact to check.

We got our grades back – I really had prepared, and got a low A. Like I said, I'm not stupid, I just can't seem to make up my mind sometimes.

I thought I'd made a clean getaway after class, and was halfway to my car when I heard someone calling my name. Without thinking, I turned, and realized too late that it was Tom Wilton.

"Hey, Jake! How'd you do on the test?"

"Oh. Hi, Tom. Pretty good. You?"

"Terrible!" He laughed and shrugged. "I suck at history."

"Yeah, it's not my best subject. I just study the hell out of it."

"Maybe I should try that. Or maybe…" He stopped and looked off towards the old science building. "Maybe Dad getting… well, maybe it got to me more than I wanted to admit."

That sounded likely – and normal. I had to admit I was kind of glad to hear he wasn't as unaffected as he had claimed before, because that had unnerved me a bit.

"I can see how that would be."

He nodded, and invited me to lunch again. I could have come up with an excuse, and I probably should have, but I didn't. My nice guy side felt bad for him, and under other circumstances I think we could have been friends. Maybe after all this was over – and if he wasn't the killer – we could be.

I asked about Murphy again. If he thought my interest in his dad's dog was strange he didn't say so. I still had occasional dreams about Murphy, but they were settling down. According to Tom, he had completely taken over Murphy's care. His mother wouldn't have anything to do with the dog, so Tom kept him in his part of the house.

"Your 'part of the house'?" My parents have money, but I couldn't see them giving me my own part of the house.

"Yeah. It's like a mother-in-law suite – you know, like a little apartment with its own bathroom and a little kitchen and its own entrance. When I started college my mom talked my dad into letting me move into it."

"That's cool, huh?"

"Yeah, I guess. I wanted to move out, but I didn't have my own money to do it with, and my dad said if I was going to go to school in the city, on his dime, I could live at home – he wasn't going to shell out money for a place for me to live when I had a perfectly good place to live already. This was a compromise. My mom said a young man my age should have some privacy and independence."

"So it works out pretty good, then?"

"Yes and no."

"How's that?"

"I think my dad figured I wanted a place to bring girls. And he probably would have been okay with that."

"But?"

"But, well… I can't believe I'm telling you this, but he found out I was bringing home guys, if you know what I mean."

"I know exactly what you mean. So, dad wasn't cool with that, I take it?"

"Not by a long shot. I think he would have kicked me out altogether if it hadn't been for Mom."

"Go Mom, right?"

"Mom's, well… she's my mom. She loves me no matter what. They had a huge fight. She looks all cool and classy when she's dressed up, but she curses like a drunk biker when she gets angry. Dad hates – hated – when anyone stood up to him. He was one of those guys who always wanted to get his way. I think relations were still chilly between them when he… died…"

His voice faded off, and I wondered if he was realizing what he'd told me – that his mom and dad had been fighting and she may have had a motive. There was no way I couldn't tell Petreski this, and if Petreski started asking questions, Tom would know who his source was. I should have stayed at home.

❧

"So let me get this straight. You had lunch with Tom Wilton again?" Petreski did not sound happy. I knew he wouldn't be, but he seemed to be fixated on me having lunch with Tom, not on the juicy details of marital strife in the Wilton home.

"Yeah, but that's not the point."

"I get the point, but why are you having lunch with Tom Wilton when you… when you know you're supposed to be staying out of trouble and not talking to suspects or witnesses?"

"Um… well…" And then it hit me. "You're jealous!"

"What? I'm not jealous! Why on earth would you say that?"

"You so *are*! I told you Tom Wilton flirted with me the other day, and that *very* evening you showed up on my doorstep. Like you were calling dibs or staking a claim. Oh my gosh! That's it, isn't it? That's exactly what you were doing!"

He didn't say anything, and even though I couldn't see his face I bet he looked pissed off. I looked over to where Don was sitting at the other end of his sofa. He had forgiven me – we could never stay mad at each other for more than a few hours – but he didn't look pleased about me having lunch with Tom Wilton, either.

"Detective Petreski – Ruben? Are you still there?"

"I'm here." It sounded like he was gritting his teeth. So sexy.

"I don't mind if you're jealous. Or, you know, worried about me."

There was silence, and I decided to wait him out this time. After a few seconds he sighed. "Of course I'm worried. There's a murderer out there, and you keep winding up in the middle of things. You get accosted in the coffee shop, threatened, warned off, and then the victim's son – who is a suspect, don't forget – starts trying to cozy up to you. How could I not be worried?"

"And maybe, a little jealous?"

"Fine. Maybe a little, okay? But it's not like I can do anything about that right now, and you know why. So if you'd just… I don't know…"

"Give you a break and try to behave myself?"

"Yes, that. And whatever you do, don't go over to Tom Wilton's love nest."

"Love nest? Just how old *are* you, anyway?"

"I'm thirty-three, if you must know. And don't go to the Wiltons' house."

"Well, I hadn't planned to, but why? I mean, I've been really open and given you all the scoop – every little detail. If someone says hello to me while I'm walking down the street you hear about it. So if I'm supposed to stay away, can I at least know why?"

He sighed again. "Okay, look. Between us, right? And Don, because I know you'll tell him and he's probably sitting there anyway."

"Promise."

"Helena Wilton has a gambling problem. Her so-called spa weekends are really spent at casinos in Louisiana. She's addicted to high-stakes poker, and she recently lost big. Clarence's death makes her a very wealthy widow with no one to answer to."

"Oh."

"So Tom may or may not know about his mother's money issues, but put what he told you about his parents' fight on top of that…"

"Yeah. I get it."

"Good. So remember what I said, okay?"

"Okay. But try to wrap this up soon, yeah?"

"Yeah."

I told Don what Petreski had told me about Helena Wilton's gambling problem, and we spent a few minutes talking about what we had learned, and that's when Don said the smartest thing he'd said all week.

"We need to do internet searches on these people."

"Who? Which ones?"

"All of them. Everyone connected to this. The Wiltons. The Katzes, Harry, Dawn Thrasher. If she's the kind of activist troublemaker Jennifer Katz and Harry describe, there's probably all kinds of stuff about her online and in newspaper archives and stuff."

"Makes sense. I'll go get my laptop. You make a list of everybody we need to look up."

❧

We had varying degrees of success. We found some old newspaper stories about the demonstrations that had gotten Harry in trouble. There was even a grainy photo of Dawn holding up a sign, and what looked like a young Harry standing next to her. And as far as we could tell, everything else Harry had said was true. There were no other stories or records about him. There was some stuff in the local news and business journal about him opening Ground Up, but nothing that had anything to do with protests, or Wilton, or property developments in general.

There wasn't much on Tom Wilton, either. We figured he was just too young to have much of an online presence beyond his social media accounts. He was more discreet with his pictures and posts than most people his age. Maybe I was right, and he didn't have many friends. That was sad.

Helena Wilton, on the other hand, was all over the internet. She didn't have any social media accounts that we could find, but she was a staple in the local press and society sites. She was on the boards of museums, hospitals, foundations, and charities. She was a fixture at galas and fundraisers. Readers wanted to know what she was wearing, and wanted to talk about it. What was most interesting to me, though, was that in all those photographs she was alone, or standing with other board members or event organizers or celebrity guests. I only saw one picture of her with Clarence. She was smiling, although it looked brittle and didn't reach her eyes, and he was looking off to one side, completely disengaged. I was starting to get the impression that Clarence and Helena lived separate lives under the same roof.

But we also learned something else very interesting about Helena. I started wondering, if Clarence had no interest in his wife's good works, was he funding them? It seemed unlikely, based on what we had learned about his personality. So I started delving deeper into Helena's background. I even poked around on one of those genealogy websites. It turned out she had a rich uncle – literally. Helena was an only child, but her mother had come from a large family and there was a whole passel of cousins. Her mother's brother Liam, though, had died single and childless, and it had been a family scandal when he left his entire fortune to Helena.

There were court records where the cousins had contested the will, but they got nothing. Uncle Liam and his lawyers had known what they were doing, and Helena had inherited over fifty million dollars, the details of which were made embarrassingly public in the court records. Twenty million in a charitable trust – the proceeds of which Helena could donate as she saw fit. The remainder went into a trust for her personal use, and she would receive a monthly payment. It sounded similar to my own trust, only much, much larger. If her payouts were what I guessed, then all she'd need to do was wait until next month's check cleared and she could pay off her gambling debts.

"But what about Clarence?" Don asked.

"What about him?"

"Wouldn't part of that money be his? Texas is a community property state, and she got that after they were married."

"No, it says here she inherited it as her own, separate property. That means Clarence would have no claim and no control over it or what she did with it. So she could use her allowance to pay off her debts and he'd never know."

"So it's not likely she'd need to kill Clarence off for his money, then. But wouldn't the police have figured this out already?"

"Not if they haven't gotten her financial records yet. Maybe that takes time. Maybe they're going through channels or whatever, and that takes longer than snooping on the internet."

"Or maybe her debts are staggering."

"Maybe." I wasn't sure I could picture her losing control to that extent, gambling addiction or not.

"But yeah, if she didn't need the money, what does that mean? Would that clear her?" Don asked.

"Not necessarily. She could have another motive. They'd fought over Tom. Who knows what else they might have fought about?"

"So we haven't really gotten anywhere."

"I wouldn't say that – we've learned a lot about Helena. And we still have the Katzes and Dawn Thrasher to check out."

Jennifer Katz was another bust. My first thought was that she must have no life, not a ridiculous thought considering her husband. But then I remembered how she seemed to know everyone at Ground Up the other morning. Someone that outgoing would have to have some kind of social outlet. I found her on a social network for knitters. I had to join to find and read her posts, but it was free. She belonged to a lot of groups and had a lot of online friends. There were groups for every interest, and I could see a list of her group memberships on her public profile page – she belonged to groups for knitting sweaters, knitting shawls, favorite yarns, designers, local groups, shops she liked, TV shows, yoga, and bands. There weren't any pictures of her, but she had posted pictures of things she had made. I didn't know anything about knitting, but they looked impressive to me, and her online friends raved about them.

But being an obsessive knitter didn't make someone a murderer, even if she did carry around a bag full of pointy sticks everywhere she went.

"Don?"

"Yeah?"

"Did we ever find out how Clarence Wilton was killed?"

"Well, we reckon he was stabbed, right?"

"Yeah, but for sure? Do we know?"

"I don't think so. Let's see if it's in the news." Don started searching the local paper and TV news sites for reports, and I started thinking more about someone who carried pointy sticks around everywhere they went. Or people who might have access to such a collection.

"Says he was stabbed. Why?"

"They wouldn't say, though, what he was stabbed with, would they?"

Don shook his head. "No. Doesn't say. But the police wouldn't give out that much detail, would they?"

"I wouldn't think so."

"Why?"

"I was wondering how hard it would be to stab someone with a knitting needle."

"Well, I guess it depends. What are knitting needles made out of?"

I thought about my cruise through Jennifer Katz' favorite site. "Just about anything. Wood, bamboo, metal, plastic."

"Then I guess, if it's pointy enough and you're strong enough, sure, you could kill someone with a knitting needle. You don't think Jennifer Katz could do it, though, do you?"

"I don't know. But I could see Josh Katz doing it. And maybe he could swipe a knitting needle from his wife's collection, clean it, and get it back before she notices it's gone."

"I could see that happening."

"Are you searching on Katz now?"

"Yeah. He's got a temper, and it's gotten him in trouble in the past. He also has a tendency to get into flame wars online. He's kind of a troll."

"Why am I not surprised? I'll start searching on Dawn."

Wow. Dawn Thrasher sure did get around. Harry knew her at the beginning of her career, before she really got going. Lucky for him he got out when he did.

We must have lost track of time, because I heard a scratching at Don's door and a black paw was waving around beneath the door.

"Oh! It's Boo!" I said, getting up. "Does he come visit you, too?" I felt a little less special at that thought.

"Nope." Don shook his head. "He must have known you were over here – heard your voice or smelled you."

"Boo!" I said, opening the door so the regal black cat could come in. "Were you looking for me?"

I let Boo investigate for a minute and greet Bridger while I gathered up my computer and other stuff. "We'll finish up tomorrow?" I asked Don, who nodded.

"Okay, Boo. Let's go to my place, huh? I haven't had dinner yet. Come on, okay?"

I headed for the door and Boo followed me back to my place. I put some water down for him and dug around in the refrigerator for some leftovers to heat up.

"How was your day, Boo? Huh?"

Boo meowed, but he didn't sound like he was complaining.

"That's good, I guess. I had class, and then I had lunch with Tom Wilton again. That kind of got me in trouble."

Boo trilled.

"Yeah, with that hunky detective I was telling you about. But I can't help it, Boo. People just talk to me. I guess I have one of those faces. I mean, you come over and talk to me, right?"

Boo rubbed against my legs and thwacked me with his tail.

"Maybe you should go back across the hall and visit with Bridger, Boo. I have to study and I won't be very good company. Huh?"

I sat down, putting my dinner plate on the coffee table and picking up a book. "See, Boo? I have to read this tonight. Not a fun time for a cat."

Boo looked at the book, cocking his head, and I imagined him trying to read the title. He curled up next to me, and I took that to mean he wasn't going anywhere, for the moment at least. I stuffed some chicken in my mouth and started reading.

☙

I had another dream that night. But it wasn't about Murphy this time. Or rather, I wasn't Murphy this time. I really needed to go see Miss Nancy again. Anyway, this time I felt different. With Murphy I felt light and curious and excited. This time I felt thick and heavy. I didn't want to run and explore. I was curled up, warm and cozy. But someone, or something, was making me leave my spot and go outside. I wasn't scared, just resentful.

Boo woke me up again. I must have been tossing and turning. "Sorry, Boo. It's okay – nothing scary this time. Thanks for waking me up, though." I kissed the top of his silky head and went back to sleep.

Perez Has a Soft Spot

TUESDAY MORNING Don and I were back at Ground Up. And Bridger, of course. Bridger stuck his head out of the sling and looked around the shop, but seemed content to stay put. His eyes were turning a golden color that reminded me of the lady cat Boo had brought with him the other day.

Somehow we managed to drink our coffee and eat our pastries without encountering anyone, other than Harry, of course, but he was too busy to talk.

"I want to go over to the pet store and buy a leash and harness for Bridger. Do you want to come?"

"Sure, why not. I'll look at the birds or something."

We walked again, enjoying the cool weather while it lasted. Don headed off to look for a harness and I tried to get the grumpy parrot in the bird section to talk to me. I tried getting my mind to relax, like the time I had "known" Raymond's name. I'd heard parrots were intelligent, so I thought maybe I'd get some useful information. Mostly he was sad because he was stuck in a cage. I didn't blame him for not wanting to talk, and moved on.

I caught up with Don as he was heading for the aisle with cat treats. We turned the corner and there – holding a bag of treats and reading the ingredients with a scowl on her face – was Detective Perez. She looked up as we approached, and at least her scowl didn't get any worse.

"Um, hi, Detective Perez," I said, trying a little wave.

"Mr. Hillebrand. And Mr…?"

"Olson. Don Olson. Do you have a cat, Detective Perez?"

She looked down at the bag in her hand, then put it back on the shelf. "No, not… not at the moment."

"Oh. Well, I just got one. Maybe you could recommend a good brand of cat treats?"

She looked back at the shelf. "I don't know. They're all full of preservatives and chemicals. These aren't bad, I guess." She took a bag down and looked at it. "Yeah, these I think." She handed the bag to Don.

"Thanks. He's still pretty young, you think these'll be okay? Hey, you want to meet him? Here." He reached into the cat sling and pulled out Bridger, who blinked at the detective with his almost-golden eyes.

Detective Perez looked almost sweet as she cooed over the kitten. "He's *yours*?" She asked Don, which struck me as an odd question, but didn't faze Don.

"Yeah. I've only had him for a week. We – well, Jake, really – found him."

She looked at me. "You didn't want him?" she asked. Wow, judgy much? Was she going to give me the stink eye because I didn't adopt Bridger myself?

"Bridger is Don's. That was obvious from the very beginning. They belong together."

She squinted at me with her light brown eyes, then turned back to Don. "Can I hold him?"

"Sure! He loves meeting new people."

Watching Detective Perez cuddle Bridger in the aisle of the pet superstore had to be one of the most surreal experiences of my life, and that included the last week. Perez handed Bridger back to Don, who tucked him safely away in his sling.

"You don't have a pet, Mr. Hillebrand?" she asked me. I remembered Petreski telling me that he and Perez had talked about me, and I wondered what, exactly, he had told her.

"No. I have a friend who's a cat, and a squirrel who spies on me."

"Huh?"

"There's a big black cat who comes by my apartment and hangs out, but he's not mine. And there's a squirrel who lives in the tree outside my building. He sits on the windowsill and watches me through the window."

"He'd probably lose interest if you'd stop feeding him," Don apparently felt the need to tell me. Again.

"Maybe. But sunflower seeds are his favorite."

"How would you know that?" Perez asked. So Petreski hadn't told her *everything*.

"I just… I can just tell. Anyway, we're probably keeping you from important police business. We'll just be going and let you, um, get back to whatever… yeah, okay. Come on, Don." I grabbed Don's elbow and steered him towards the front of the store.

"Bye, Detective!" Don called over his shoulder as I dragged him away. "What the hell, Jake? That was so rude, and Detective Perez is so nice."

"The what, you say? Detective Perez hates me. She's mean and kind of scary."

"No. I totally don't see that at all."

"No, I guess not. But she was asking about stuff that was getting into a weird area for me, and I needed to get the hell out of there. Okay?"

"Yeah, okay. I think maybe her cat died and she feels sad. You think that's why she said she didn't have a cat 'at the moment'?"

That didn't feel like the right explanation, but since I didn't have a better answer – one that made sense – I shrugged. "Maybe."

❧

"I'm going to see Miss Nancy this afternoon. You want to come?"

Don rolled his eyes.

"A simple 'no' would suffice. You don't have to be rude."

"Sorry."

"Anyway, what with everything that's going on, I want to talk to her. And I thought you might be a little more open-minded after… you know. And you could always just hang at the market or something if you can't bring yourself to go inside."

"I don't know." We were crossing the bridge where we'd found Bridger, and Don stopped to look down at the water below. This was progress.

"I know she'd like to meet you."

"Yeah? Like how you knew where Bridger was and how that squirrel's name is Raymond?"

"No, because she said she wants to meet you. I've known her even longer than I've known you, and she thinks it's strange you've never met."

"Oh."

"It's not all psychic powers and mind-reading and the power of the Tarot, you know."

"Sorry."

I shrugged.

"Can I bring Bridger?"

"Yeah, I think she'd probably like to meet him, too. She's got a soft spot for cats."

"I'll think about it."

Jake Buys Don a Candle

DON DID go with me to see Miss Nancy that afternoon. I had a feeling Don would like Miss Nancy once he got to know her and saw that she wasn't a charlatan. For me, Miss Nancy had always been a source of common sense, good advice, and comfort. How could anyone object to that?

Miss Nancy was thrilled that I brought Don, and she fussed over and cuddled Bridger until I was afraid Don would have trouble getting him back from her. The three of us sat around Miss Nancy's kitchen table, and in honor of the occasion she got out her nice tea set.

"Now, honey," she said, as we waited for the tea to steep. "Tell me about the new presence in your life."

"It's funny, Miss Nancy. There's more than one."

She raised an eyebrow so high it almost disappeared under her tie-dyed turban.

"Well, there's Bridger, of course."

"Honey, Bridger doesn't count. Bridger is a new presence in Don's life, to be accurate."

"Well, there's Boo."

"Mm-hmm."

"He's this big black cat who's started coming around. It's the strangest thing. It's like he's a person, almost, we just don't speak the same language. Or at least, I don't speak cat."

I told them about the evening Boo had brought the lady cat, and how Boo had kept Bridger from trying to follow her out the window. Miss Nancy agreed that this was exceptional behavior, but didn't have an explanation for it.

"This is all mighty interesting, honey, but please get to the point."

"The point?"

"You know what I'm talking about. I was there when you bought that 'Bring Love to Me' candle. And I know you probably ran straight home and lit that thing."

Don stifled a snort.

"Okay, fine. Yes, I lit it." I told her about Petreski, and how he had come over. I told her about Tom Wilton and how I thought he might like me and that Petreski was jealous.

Just like always, Miss Nancy sipped her tea and let me talk. Miss Nancy didn't have to even try to be a psychic with me – I always told her everything. But she could piece things together and see connections and patterns better than I could. This was what Don had never understood. I didn't go to see Miss Nancy for psychic advice. Going to see Miss Nancy was how I cleared my mind.

Miss Nancy put on her thinking face and stared at the ceiling.

"What –"

"Shh." I told Don in a whisper. "She's thinking."

After a minute Miss Nancy straightened herself, took a sip of tea and asked, "Jake, honey, did that squirrel ever tell you anything of interest?"

"Just his name."

"His name?"

"Yeah. It's Raymond. I'm afraid I offended him, but we're past that now."

"And that's all?" she asked with a smirk.

"Yeah. And that he loves sunflower seeds. They're his favorite."

"And that's really all you got out of that exchange?"

I looked over at Don, and he had the fingers of one hand over his mouth, like he knew the answer to this question and was trying to keep himself from blurting it out. What was I missing?

"Dude…" Don looked over at Miss Nancy, and she nodded. "Dude, think about it. How do you know these things? I mean, think about *how* you found out."

"Raymond told me."

"And Raymond is…"

"Raymond is a – shit. I don't mean Raymond is a shit. Sorry, Miss Nancy. I mean, Raymond is a freaking squirrel. Yeah, right. I had a meltdown over it the night it happened. It was when Petreski came over and he kind of forced me into figuring out what I am."

"And Detective Petreski didn't seem shocked by what happened?" Miss Nancy asked.

"No. He had told me – that day we all walked over to the bridge. He told me that he has a high tolerance for the unusual. I figured he meant because he's a cop he's seen all kinds of crazy stuff in his work. Maybe that's not exactly what he meant."

"Maybe you should ask him."

"Maybe, but I can't. At least, not until the case is solved."

"Are you frightened?"

"Frightened?"

"When we talked about this the last time you were here, you wondered whether the things that were happening were your fault."

I heard Don make a surprised noise, but I didn't take my eyes off Miss Nancy. "I'm not worried about that anymore."

"No. And we talked about how most people find out about this kind of thing when they're younger."

"Petreski had a theory about that. He thinks I've always had a connection with animals, but it was never able to develop because I never had a pet when I was a kid, or formed a bond with an animal until I started feeding Raymond."

"That makes Raymond very special, you know."

"It does?"

"Yes. I think, the more you develop your bond with Raymond, the more you'll learn about what you are and what you can do."

"Maybe. It can't hurt to try."

"And ask your Detective Petreski. He may know more than he's told you so far."

We all sipped our tea, thinking.

"What about Boo, Miss Nancy?"

"I don't know… There's something I can't quite put my finger on. I need to think on him some more."

After another minute of silent tea drinking, Don finally spoke up.

"Did you… did you really think all this stuff might be your fault?"

"I didn't know… was I dreaming something that had already happened, or was stuff happening because I was dreaming it? I didn't know what was happening, and I was scared."

"What about now?"

"I still have a lot of questions, but I'm not scared. And I'm still having dreams, but they're not scary anymore. No one's gotten killed in them. And Boo's been waking me up when they start."

"I don't know that that's such a good thing," said Miss Nancy.

"What do you mean?"

"Some of these dreams might be important. There might be things in them you need to know. This might sound crazy. But try asking him to let you sleep through your dreams unless they get really bad and you're in distress."

"But, he's a cat."

"He's not a normal cat."

"No, he's not. I'll try."

We took Miss Nancy to the market and botanica after that. I bought a Road Opener candle for Don, and I think he appreciated it even though he rolled his eyes. Miss Nancy picked out some herbs and mixed up a tea blend for me. It was supposed to help me think clearly and make decisions. I told her about my disastrous attempt to smoke the, um, herb she had given me the last time, and about how Petreski had smoked the rest of it, and she laughed so hard she had to wipe her eyes. At least someone was amused.

A Guy Can't Even Get a Beer

I THOUGHT I'd feel silly, asking a cat not to wake me up if I had a bad dream, but Boo looked at me like he understood, and head-butted me when I'd finished. Talking to Boo was not like talking to a cat. My life had gotten so strange.

That night I dreamed about the heavy mind again. I tried to pay more attention this time, to figure out what I was, where I was, anything. I was a dog – I could sense that much. I stretched, and I felt powerful. Murphy had felt light and agile – which made sense because he was a terrier. This time I felt strong, but that was it. I could hear voices, but I couldn't make out what they were saying. There was a deep voice that made me prick up my ears. That voice made me feel strange. I was afraid, and confused.

There was another voice, higher-pitched. This voice sounded afraid, too. I whined. I needed to protect. The voices were on the other side of a door, and I couldn't get to them. I tried to speak, and heard a low-pitched bark. I tried again, a little louder. The voices stopped for a moment, and then the deep voice started speaking again, louder and faster.

I sensed anger and fear from the other side of the door, and that fueled my own fear. I needed to help, but didn't know how. A part of me was still Jake, but unable to do anything but observe. I had no control over the body or consciousness I was inhabiting.

I woke up then, on my own. I turned, and Boo was watching me, tail twitching, but not touching me. "Hey, Boo," I croaked, my throat dry. I got up to get a glass of water. Boo followed me into the kitchen, not taking his eyes off of me.

"I'm okay, Boo," I told him after I'd drunk some water. "Thanks for letting me sleep – you did good." I ran my hand down his back and he pressed up against my touch.

I went back to bed and Boo hopped up next to me.

"Somebody's in trouble, Boo. I think I know who, but I don't know how to do anything about it."

❧

I poured myself a cup of coffee, put a handful of sunflower seeds on the windowsill, and waited. After a minute Raymond showed up, nose twitching, and looking around.

"Boo's gone, Raymond. Don't worry, though – he won't hurt you, I promise."

Moving slowly, I shifted from the sofa to sit on the edge of the coffee table. "Raymond – is it okay if I call you Ray?" He cocked his head at me and I couldn't sense any negative vibes, so I took that as a yes.

"Thanks. So, I'm Jake, by the way. I guess we haven't actually been introduced. I'm not sure, well, this is new for me, okay? So if you'll be patient with me, I'll try not to screw up too much."

Raymond kept eating, so I kept talking.

"See, Miss Nancy, she's a friend of mine. Anyway, she figures you're probably special. Like, you and I have a bond or something. And that I should try to get to know you better. I've never known a squirrel before, though. Do squirrels have friends, Ray?"

He looked at me, blinking and chewing.

"My friend Don, he lives across the hall. You've seen him before, right? He's kind of afraid of squirrels, but I've told him you're okay. He's afraid you'll try to come inside, but I'm not worried. I mean, if you wanted to come in, I'd be okay with that as long as you tried not to mess anything up."

Raymond cocked his head at me, then placed one front paw through the window, moving it from the brick ledge outside to the wooden sill inside. He held his other front paw curled against his chest, ready to dash if I made any sudden moves.

I sat as still as I could and slowly raised my coffee cup to take a sip, never breaking my gaze on Raymond. His other paw came down, and he hopped onto the inner sill and sat up, looking around.

Keeping my voice soft, I started speaking again. "See, it's okay. Nothing scary. Although, you might not want to come in when Bridger is over. He's pretty small still, and might not understand. He might try to play rough or something, and I wouldn't want either one of you to get hurt. It'll have to be a judgment call on your part, but the main thing is that he doesn't get hurt, okay? Because he's still a baby."

Raymond cocked his head and twitched his tail. I caught a sense of understanding, and wondered whether it was real or my imagination. I hoped that, in time, I'd learn to tell the difference.

❧

Tom Wilton wasn't in class that day. I wondered whether he was at home, finally grieving for his father, or just slacking off. Whatever the reason for his absence, I was relieved not to have to deal with him again.

Don was out when I got home, and I remembered he was working the lunch shift today. I fixed myself a sandwich, raised the window in case

Raymond felt like visiting, and settled in to get some reading done while I waited for Don to get home.

Raymond didn't show, but I heard Don get in around two-thirty. It really was true that you couldn't come and go without being heard. I decided to give Don time to clean up and greet Bridger. If he didn't come by before too long I'd go over there and get him. I wanted to tell him about Boo, and my dream, and Raymond. Also, I wanted to find out if he'd lit his candle. He probably wouldn't tell me, though, so maybe I'd have to go over there and poke around.

Twenty minutes later I knocked on Don's door. He cracked it open and looked out at me with one eye. "What?"

"What? What do you mean, what? I've got stuff to tell you. Why are you acting weird?"

"I'm not acting weird."

"Then why aren't you opening the door?"

"I don't want Bridger to get out."

"How long did you practice that line? Come on, let me in."

Don sighed and stepped back. When I walked into his apartment I could see right into the kitchen and the Road Opener candle was flickering away on the stove top. "A-ha!"

"Whatever. I figured it couldn't hurt. Besides, it looks nice."

I didn't say anything else – I didn't want to seem smug. "You wanna get a beer at Ground Up?"

"Yeah, sure."

I waited while he put Bridger in his sling, then put the harness, leash, and treats in his backpack. I didn't ask, I figured I'd find out soon enough.

We sat on the patio sipping our beers and I told Don about the events of the previous night and that morning. He was not impressed by my inviting Raymond inside for a chat, but didn't give me a hard time about it.

When Bridger started stirring, Don took him out of the sling and put the harness on him. Bridger was not thrilled, but didn't fight it. Don hooked the leash to the harness, and gave Bridger a treat. Bridger had no objection to the treat.

"Are you going to put him down on the ground?" I asked.

"Not yet. Right now I'm just getting him used to wearing it. If he starts getting restless I'll put him down and see what happens."

It was a perfect moment. The sun was bright and warm, the breeze was cool, and the beer was cold. We were relaxing and enjoying the peace and quiet when Harry came outside, a phone pressed to his ear.

"Yes. Yes, I understand. I'll be here." He ended the call and turned to go back inside. Don and I looked at each other and shrugged. Something was going on, and I didn't really want to know.

Don's phone rang, and I got a funny feeling.

"Hello? Yes. He's right here, hang on." He passed his phone over to me. "It's Detective Petreski."

I took the phone, but I had a feeling this wasn't a social call. "Hello?"

"Jake. Where are you right now?"

"We're at Ground Up. On the patio."

"Is anyone else out there with you?"

I looked around. "No. Harry was just out here talking on the phone, but he went back inside. He was talking to you, wasn't he?"

"Yes. Stay there, okay? Don't leave, and don't talk to anyone. We'll be there soon."

"What's going on?"

"Just sit tight. I'll explain when we get there. Five minutes. Okay?"

"Okay."

I handed the phone back to Don. "We're supposed to stay here and not talk to anybody until they get here."

"What's going on?"

"He said he'd tell us when he gets here. But I've got a bad feeling it has to do with that dream I had last night."

A few minutes later I saw a dark sedan pull into an empty space and Petreski and Perez got out. They looked towards us, and Perez sneered at me, nodded to Don, and turned to go inside. Petreski walked towards our table.

"Have you talked to anyone? Anyone at all since the last time we spoke?"

Don shook his head.

"No. Tom Wilton wasn't even in class today."

Petreski looked around, then pulled a chair over to sit down.

"Dawn Thrasher is dead."

That was not what I was expecting to hear.

"Wh… Dawn Thrasher? *Dawn Thrasher* is dead?" I was thinking about the searches Don and I had done, and how we hadn't gotten far with Dawn when we quit for the evening. Had we made a mistake, not going back and finishing?

Petreski was looking at me, head cocked to one side. "What's wrong?"

Don waved a hand in front of my face. "Jake? You okay? Is this what you dreamed last night?"

I shook my head.

"What did you dream last night?" Petreski asked.

"It was… there were two people, a man and a woman. I was in the house with them, but in a different room and I couldn't get to them or make out what they were saying."

"Was the woman Dawn Thrasher?"

"No. The woman in the dream was afraid. Dawn wouldn't have been afraid of anything or anyone. I think it was Jennifer Katz."

"The bulldog," Petreski said. I nodded.

Petreski took out his phone and pushed a speed dial button. "Yeah. Send a car to the Katz residence. I need a welfare check on Jennifer Katz. If she's there, ask her to go to Ground Up with you, and bring the dog with her. Call me back."

"Could you get a sense of anything from the dog?"

"He was afraid and confused by Josh, and protective towards Jennifer. I think he's really her dog, at least in his mind. The more afraid Jennifer got, the more agitated the dog became. When… how… did Dawn? Was she killed, or…"

"It was not natural causes, if that's what you're asking."

"Was it like Wilton?"

"I can't say, I'm sorry." He sounded like he really was sorry.

"Wilton was stabbed, wasn't he?"

"Yes. That much was released."

"But do you know with what? Was it a knife, or something more, well, pointy?"

"What's pointier than a knife?"

"I mean, something without a blade. Just a point."

He looked at me for a minute, and then asked, his tone neutral. "What makes you ask that?"

"Jennifer Katz has – probably has – a huge collection of knitting needles. I got to thinking, one could go missing and she might not notice for days. Or one could get borrowed. And here's the thing. If someone had walked up to Clarence Wilton with a knife in his – or her – hand, he would have been scared. But he wasn't, at least not at first. He was angry, but not afraid."

I looked over at Don, who was nodding in agreement.

Petreski pulled his phone out again and dialed a number. "It's Petreski. Yeah – Clarence Wilton. Listen, could a knitting needle do the job? Check it out, and let me know. Do it quick as you can, I'll need to get a warrant if so."

He disconnected and looked back and forth between Don and me. "Okay. Anything else?"

"Are you mad?"

"I'm not mad, but I wish you weren't so interested in this case."

"I can't help it. I didn't ask to dream about it in the first place."

"I know, I'm sorry. Seriously, though. Is there anything else?"

I looked at Don. Let him take this one.

"Helena Wilton has her own money."

Petreski raised an eyebrow. "And you know this how?"

"Internet."

Don wasn't explaining this well, so I jumped in. "We looked her up online. She's a major philanthropist. I figured, Clarence probably wouldn't fund stuff like that, so we dug a little deeper. It's all in public court records. She inherited a fortune from an uncle and the will was contested. If she has gambling debts, all she has to do is pay them off from her trust fund allowance. She wouldn't need Clarence's money."

Petreski growled and pulled out his phone again. "Petreski. Put Hastings on the line. Now." He glared and tapped his foot. I was glad I wasn't Hastings. "Yeah. Petreski. Tell me about Helena Wilton's trust fund. The inheritance from her uncle? Apparently, you don't need to wait for financials. Apparently, it's in public records. Yes, on the internet. Do you have an internet connection, Hastings? Yeah? Try using it. Try not sending us out here with half-assed information that makes us look like half-assed cops." He cut the call and grinned at us. "That felt good. Hastings is useless."

I took a big swig of my beer. That grin was unnerving.

"Please tell me that's everything. I don't want to make any more phone calls."

"I can't think of anything. You, Don?"

Don shook his head. Bridger mewed and Petreski looked down at the kitten in his harness.

"Oh, geez. Perez has *got* to see this."

Petreski's phone rang and he frowned down at it before answering. "Petreski. Yeah? Good. Ground Up, on Studewood. Bring her – them – to the patio. Thanks."

"Do you want us to leave?" Don asked.

"No, believe it or not, I don't. Just sit here and look like you're minding your own business. Jake, I want you to pay attention to the dog. If you sense anything from him, ask Don to go get you another beer. Don, if he sends you inside, find Perez and tell her I need her out here, got it?" We nodded, and he moved to another table to wait for Jennifer Katz.

A black and white squad car pulled up a minute later, and an officer escorted Jennifer Katz over to where Petreski was sitting. She glanced over and recognized us, but her attention went immediately back to Petreski as she sat, reaching one hand down to pet the bulky dog at her side.

"What's your dog's name, Mrs. Katz?" Petreski asked.

"Buttercup." She smiled down at the dog when he woofed at the sound of his name. "He's a good boy, aren't you? Yes."

I tried to relax and focus on the dog, but I felt ridiculous. "I feel ridiculous," I said to Don.

"Shut up and focus."

"Oh, thanks. That was really helpful."

Petreski was asking her about her husband, and where he'd been recently. She claimed she didn't know anything about any contact or relationship with Wilton, although she did admit that Katz was upset about Wilton's development activities in the neighborhood. When Petreski asked about Dawn Thrasher, though, I could sense the dog's agitation go through the roof. Mrs. Katz looked calm, but he had to be picking up on her emotions. She put her hand down to pet the dog, and he calmed. She must have calmed as well.

"Hey, Don, would you go grab me another beer?"

"Sure." Don got up and headed inside.

A few minutes later, Perez came out and approached the table where Petreski was sitting with Mrs. Katz. Petreski stood, Perez took his seat, and Petreski came over to where I was sitting.

"What?"

"When you asked her about Dawn Thrasher, she looked calm, but I think she was freaking out on the inside, because the dog started freaking. Then she put her hand down and the dog relaxed. I know she knows – or knows about – Dawn. When I described her the other day, Mrs. Katz knew who she was immediately, and didn't want to talk about her."

"Right."

He went back over to the other table and pulled over a third chair for himself.

"Mrs. Katz," I heard him say. "I really need you to tell me everything you know about Dawn Thrasher."

"I don't… I don't know her well. We've only met a few times. She's come to some of our meetings, and talked about ways to demonstrate and make a fuss about what Wilton was doing in the neighborhood. But that's all the contact I really had with her. She's too, well, aggressive I think. Like everything is a battle to be fought and won. It's tiring to be around someone like that."

"Someone like your husband?" Perez interjected.

"I beg your pardon?"

"Your husband has a history of similar behavior, I believe. And there have been some calls from neighbors – shouting and loud noises coming from your house. Is there something you'd like to tell us, Mrs. Katz? Jennifer?" Perez actually sounded sympathetic.

"I don't… what are you getting at?"

Petreski glanced over at me and I nodded. The agitation was ratcheting up again. There was definitely something here.

"Mrs. Katz, what Detective Perez and I need to know is whether you have any reason to believe that your husband may have been planning any kind of activity with Ms. Thrasher. Anything that might have led to trouble? Ms. Thrasher's reputation is one of violent activism. Would your husband have been convinced or lured into participating in anything like that?"

I could feel some of the tension ease. This was not what she was hiding.

"Oh, no. Nothing like that. Josh is, well, he's got a temper, but I can't see him plotting anything devious, if that's what you mean."

Petreski glanced over again, and I shook my head. They were on the wrong track.

"How did Ms. Thrasher come to be involved in your organization? Did she ever say what brought her to Houston, or what got her involved in this particular issue?"

"Well, I think someone in the group knew about her. They had heard of the work she was doing in other neighborhoods and invited her to speak to us about ways to protest and get results. I remember – oh, who was it?" She paused for a minute. "Carl Burke – that's who it was. He found her online and sent her an email. He said she wasn't interested at first, but once she found out it was Clarence Wilton we were up against she jumped at the offer."

Perez was taking notes, and Petreski was nodding, encouraging Mrs. Katz to go on. "That's great. So no one else in the group knew Ms. Thrasher before she got here, as far as you know?"

"That's right."

"What about after the talk she gave? Were people interested? Did she form any alliances or associations that you know of?"

The dog was completely calm now. Whatever had Mrs. Katz upset earlier had little, if anything, to do with Dawn Thrasher's professional activities. I wondered why Don hadn't come back with my beer, when Harry came around the corner with a bottle in his hand. He put it on the table in front of me. "Don'll be back in a minute."

"Okay. Thanks, Harry."

Watching Harry walk away it dawned on me. Dawn Thrasher was the girl who had gotten Harry mixed up in her mess all those years ago. Dawn and Harry… Dawn who had a new man in a matter of days… Dawn Thrasher, who didn't do anything that didn't further her cause, and likewise would do whatever she had to do. Dawn Thrasher would have become more focused, and more ruthless, as she got older. Dawn Thrasher, manipulator and user of men.

I choked on the swallow of beer I had just taken at that thought. Ew. The bubbles burned my nose and I gasped for breath. I knew Perez was probably scowling at me. I felt a hand slapping my back and I wiped my mouth and nose with the napkin that was thrust into my hand. I looked up to see Petreski frowning down at me.

"Sex," I managed to whisper when I caught my breath.

"What?!"

"Dawn… Dawn Thrasher." I choked again. "I think she probably seduced Josh Katz. She manipulates people – men – like she did Harry years ago."

Petreski nodded and straightened up. "You're sure you're all right, sir?" he asked, I assumed for Mrs. Katz's benefit.

"Oh, yes. Thank you. I'll be fine."

The tension shot right back up when they started asking about her husband's relationship with Dawn Thrasher. She claimed she didn't know anything about a relationship, and that may have been true. But she had her suspicions, I was sure of it. They didn't get very far with that line of questioning, though.

I could feel the dog tensing up again, but the source of agitation was different this time. It was the same uneasy fear I had felt in the dream last night, and a few seconds later, Josh Katz came around the corner.

"What's going on here?" he bellowed.

"Good afternoon, Mr. Katz," Petreski said, standing to greet the new arrival. "Would you care to join us?"

"No, I would not care to join you. What the devil are you playing at, questioning my wife?"

"We're just trying to establish the nature of Dawn Thrasher's role in the community's protests against Clarence Wilton."

"Then ask Dawn Thrasher. Leave my wife out of this."

"Dawn Thrasher is dead." Perez's voice was cold.

If Jennifer Katz wasn't genuinely shocked at this news, then she was a hell of an actress. Josh Katz didn't look shocked as much as angry. His face turned an astonishing shade of red.

"Mr. Katz? Are you all right? Do you need to sit down?" Petreski pulled out a chair for the older man.

"No, I don't need to sit down! We are going home. Now!" He reached down to pull his wife to her feet and the dog started barking. The chair Mrs. Katz had been sitting in fell over and Buttercup's leash got tangled in the legs. Mr. Katz started yelling at the dog, the dog barked louder, Mrs. Katz started crying, and Petreski was trying to untangle the dog's leash.

"*Enough!*" Perez had quite a set of lungs on her, and everyone froze at the sound of her voice. I wished I'd had my phone out so I could snap a photo. Even the dog was still.

"You," she pointed at Mr. Katz. "Let go of her arm and sit. Now!"

Katz looked pissed, but did as he was told, sitting in the chair Petreski had vacated.

Petreski finished untangling Buttercup and put the chair back on its legs. He handed the leash to Mrs. Katz and she sat. Petreski pulled another chair over for himself. Perez looked around the table, but remained standing.

"I take it," she said, "that you were unaware of Ms. Thrasher's demise?"

Mrs. Katz blinked up at Perez and shook her head. "I had no idea. I thought… I thought maybe she had done something and that's what you wanted to know about."

"Mr. Katz?"

"Of course I didn't know. When did it happen? Is it in the paper?"

"It is not in the paper."

"Mr. Katz," Petreski broke in, "how well did you know the deceased?"

"She was organizing some protests for our group."

"And was that the extent of your relationship?" Perez asked.

"What do you mean, the extent?"

"Oh, for fuck's sake, Josh. They're asking if you were having an affair with her!"

Everyone turned at Jennifer Katz's uncharacteristic outburst. My own jaw fell open. The dog whined.

"Well, that's it, isn't it?"

Perez nodded, her curls bouncing. "Yes, Mrs. Katz. You seem to have cut cleanly to the chase."

"Jennifer, I think you're overwrought."

"Shut up and answer them, Josh. Do you think I'm stupid? Did you really think I didn't know? Did you think I even cared?"

"Wait… what?"

Jennifer didn't answer. She sat back in her chair and reached down to pet Buttercup. It seemed like she was done with this conversation. Maybe she was done with Josh, too. Good for her.

"Mr. Katz," Petreski said as he stood, "I think perhaps we should continue this conversation at the station?"

"I don't think so."

"You misunderstand me. It was not a request. Our car is just over here. That's right."

Katz shuffled towards the car with Perez and Petreski turned to nod at me, then spoke quietly with Jennifer before he followed them. As they pulled away, I picked up my beer and went to sit next to Jennifer. I held my fingers down for Buttercup to sniff and got a big doggy lick on the back of my hand.

"He likes you," Jennifer said.

"Dogs usually do."

"That's good. Dogs are excellent judges of character."

"Does he like Josh?"

"Can't stand him."

"And you?"

"Do I like Josh?"

"Yeah."

"Not much. Not anymore."

"I'm sorry."

"Don't be. I can't see him as a murderer, but the cheating is a good excuse to kick his sorry ass out." She shrugged. "I'm getting on with my life, just as soon as all this mess is over with."

"Yeah. Me too."

"You?"

"Yeah. I found Clarence Wilton's body, you know? And stuff just kind of keeps happening around me. And, well, there's some things I want to get on with that I can't do until the case is solved."

She nodded.

"You, uh… you want a beer or something?" I asked her.

She shook her head. "No. Thank you. I think I'm going to go home, call a locksmith, and drink a few gin and tonics while he rekeys the locks."

"Do you need a ride?"

"No. It's a lovely day for a walk. Come on, Buttercup."

She stood, nodded to me, and headed off, Buttercup waddling behind her.

I saw Don stick his head around the corner and look around before he came to join me.

"Where have you been?" I asked.

"Detective Perez told me to stay inside until they left. What happened? I heard yelling."

"Turns out Katz was having an affair with Dawn Thrasher."

"No!"

"Yes! Jennifer Katz knew about it and totally ratted him out. Petreski and Perez took Katz to the station for further discussion."

"Wow."

"So, what was Perez doing inside? Terrorizing Harry?"

"Kind of. She was asking him about Dawn Thrasher, and whether he had had any contact with her. He was telling her about Thrasher coming into the shop when I went in there."

"I think we need to go home and finish our research on Dawn."

"But why? She's dead."

"That's exactly why. I realized something while all the drama was going down out here. Dawn was the kind of person who used her sex appeal to get what she wanted. She manipulated Harry and Katz with sex. It's unlikely they were the only ones. Maybe someone else's wife *did* care. Or maybe someone got obsessed. Maybe trouble followed her here from somewhere else."

Coffee and Speculation

"SHOULD WE really be doing this?" Don asked an hour later.

"Why do you ask?"

"I mean, isn't this something the police should be doing? What if we get in trouble?"

"We're not going to get in trouble for looking up things on the internet. It's not like we're hacking into private accounts or anything. Besides, you saw what happened with Helena Wilton's trust fund. I'd say the police need all the help they can get."

News of Dawn's death hadn't broken yet, and her internet presence was huge. She had her own website, promoting her services as an organizer. The website included an online archive of press clippings going back to the beginning of her career – the older ones scanned from newspaper copy. I recognized Harry in some of the pictures from her college days.

She had traveled all over the country protesting everything from animal testing to pesticides to urban sprawl. In her younger days she had been a bit of an eco-terrorist, but she seemed to have become more mainstream as she got older.

"I would think," Don said, "that if it were a jilted lover or jealous spouse, it would have to be related to something recent. What do you think?"

"Yeah, that makes sense."

"But, how do we figure this out? I mean, it's not like she's got a list on here of who she's slept with."

"I guess we look at the most recent events. You take the most recent and I'll take the one before. We read what we can find, look for photos, see if any names or faces stand out. Like, with Harry, he was standing next to her in those pictures. See who's standing with her in the latest ones."

"It's a place to start, I guess. Then what? See what we can find out about those guys?"

"Yeah. Names, screen names, message board memberships. That kind of thing."

"An 'I slept with Dawn Thrasher' support group?"

"Seems like there ought to be one, doesn't it?"

Don snorted and we got to work.

❧

Two hours later we hadn't found anything useful and my stomach was growling.

"I'm going back to my place. I need to eat and get some studying done."

"Okay. I'll do a little more on this before I turn in. Compare notes in the morning?"

"Yeah. Not before eight, though."

I made myself a sandwich and thought about Dawn Thrasher and Clarence Wilton. If Dawn was killed by a prior conquest, or a jealous lover, what was the connection to Wilton? If any? Wouldn't it be too much of a coincidence for them to be killed within days of each other? Especially with them connected as they were. Weren't cop shows always saying that there's no such thing as coincidence? I wondered whether Petreski believed in coincidence.

Boo's polite scratch came a little later than usual that night. Cats can't tell time, so I didn't give him a hard time about being late.

"Hey, Boo," I greeted him. "Did you have a busy day, too?"

His answer was loud and sounded affirmative to me.

"Yeah. Lots of excitement for me today. You want some water?"

I put a bowl of water down for him and opened the window. It was late, so Raymond didn't show up looking for seeds.

Boo sat on the toilet lid and watched while I brushed and flossed my teeth. I wondered whether the things humans did looked strange to the animals in our lives. Cats probably didn't think about oral hygiene. I tried relaxing my mind, to see if I could pick up on Boo's emotions or sensations like I had with Buttercup, but I got nothing. Maybe cats were different, or maybe I was just tired.

"Come on, Boo. Let's go to bed."

We sprawled together on the mattress and Boo stretched out so I could rub his tummy. I had heard cats didn't like that, but Boo seemed to eat it up. We had already established, though, that Boo was not an ordinary cat.

"That scary lady got killed, Boo. Did I tell you about her? She's the one who warned me about Josh Katz, and was asking me about Wilton's dog. So weird, Boo." I yawned. "Sorry, not much… for conversation today. G'night, Boo."

I couldn't help thinking there was something I was missing, some detail I was forgetting, but I was just too tired. It would come to me. Morning would be here soon enough; I'd think about it then.

☙

When Don knocked on my door at eight sharp the next morning, I already had coffee ready and my laptop was fired up. I'd been up since six after a peaceful night's sleep. Maybe Jennifer Katz and Buttercup were sleeping soundly with new locks, or maybe Josh spent the night in jail. Murphy must be settling in with Tom. At least the dogs were worry-free.

"Did you find anything else?" I asked Don as I poured him a cup of coffee.

"No, not really. She's either been behaving herself or been really discreet the last couple of years."

"My money's on discreet. I wish we knew more about her death. Like, when or where. Was she found in the bayou, too?"

"That doesn't seem likely. I mean, when we found Wilton it was all over the message board and there were crowds. People were talking about it everywhere."

"The message board!"

"I didn't see anything about her, though."

"No, but did anyone talk about seeing police cars, or the constable or anything like that? Anything at all about any kind of suspicious activity?"

"I'll check again."

While Don logged on to the message board, I went back to Dawn Thrasher's site to see what I could find about her current project in The Heights. There was still nothing about her death on her website, which led me to believe she was a one-woman operation. Surely if she had partners they would have posted something.

"It was a quiet night. No one reported anything other than a car window smashed in Norhill."

"She must not have been staying in The Heights, then. But somewhere that she could get here quickly. Maybe Montrose or Midtown. Is there a way to check their message boards?"

"I'll find out. You see if you can figure out where she lives. I mean, are we assuming that she lived in Houston? Or that she came from out of town and was in some kind of rental or hotel?"

"Good question. I'll see what I can find out."

We both jumped when the downstairs doorbell rang.

"What the – ?"

"Who could that be?" I said. This was an old building – we didn't have intercoms or buzzers to let someone in, just doorbells to let us know someone was here. I looked out the window and saw Petreski on the porch below. "Coming!" I called out to him and he looked up and waved.

"Who is it?" Don asked.

"Petreski. I'll be right back."

"I told you we were going to get in trouble!"

"If we're in trouble it has nothing to do with this. Chill out."

I jogged down the stairs to unlock the main door. "Hey…" I said as I let him in. "Wait… How did you get in the other night?"

"You're just now worried about that?"

"Well, I was kind of distracted that evening."

"I slipped in as one of your neighbors was going out."

"What? They're not supposed to do that!"

"I flashed my badge. Don't worry about it."

"Fine. Come on up. Don and I were… well, there's coffee. What's up?"

"Hi, Detective Petreski!" Don greeted him as we entered my apartment. Don was never that perky. Way to be subtle.

"Uh, hi. Okay, what are you two up to?"

"Research," I said, pouring coffee into a mug and handing it to him. "We were curious about Dawn Thrasher."

"I should be upset, but y'all found out more about Helena Wilton in one day than my so-called expert analyst got in a week. So, spill."

"Like I said yesterday – Dawn Thrasher used sex to manipulate men. She did it to Harry years ago. It looks like she probably did it with Josh. No way were those the only instances. So we got to thinking…"

"What if she'd done it with someone whose wife or girlfriend *did* care?" Don finished.

"Yeah. So we looked at her website, and she has really complete archives. We were trying to figure out whether it looked like she had used her wiles on anyone else recently."

"Yeah. Or if there was anyone talking about her online, or obviously obsessed with her. You know, liking every post or comment she puts on Facebook, trying to start a flame war, that kind of thing."

"Did you find anything?"

Don and I shook our heads.

"We just don't have the kind of resources it takes," Don said. "Besides, if someone was sending her private messages or emails, we'd have no way of knowing."

"I'll put Hastings on it." Petreski pulled out his phone.

"Really?" I said.

"Oh yeah. He needs to redeem himself big time. This will be his chance."

Don and I exchanged looks while Petreski dialed. I felt kind of sorry for Hastings. I went back into the kitchen to start a fresh pot of coffee. A few minutes later I felt someone standing behind me. I knew it wasn't Don. At least, I really hoped it wasn't when I felt hands on my shoulders and a soft kiss was pressed against my temple.

"What was that for?" I asked. "And aren't you supposed to be keeping your distance? And why did you come over here this morning?"

He sighed and leaned his forehead against the back of my head for a moment before stepping away. "Geez, you ask a lot of questions. First, it was because I wanted to. And I am keeping my distance, but since I'm here on official business – technically – and no one else is here but Don, I thought I might get away with it."

I turned to face him. "Sorry. I'm just… worried, I guess. I just want this whole thing to be over with. I want life to be normal again."

"Sorry, Jake, but I think that ship might have sailed."

"Yeah. Well, I want to find my new normal, then."

We stood there looking at each other for a minute while the coffee dripped. I wasn't wondering whether he would be part of my new normal. Somehow I just knew.

When the coffee pot started to sputter I turned to pull it out and refill my mug. "More coffee, Don?" I called out.

"If you two can stop mooning over each other for a minute, that would be nice."

"We're not mooning," I took the pot into the main room to refill Don's mug. "But," I turned back to Petreski, "why are you –technically – officially here?"

"To follow up on yesterday's events at Ground Up." Petreski unbuttoned his suit jacket and sat on the sofa. "Such as to ask you what you discussed with Jennifer Katz after we left."

"What makes you think we discussed anything?" I put the pot back in the coffee maker and sat on the coffee table facing Don and Petreski.

"Because I left you both there knowing you wouldn't be able *not* to talk to her."

Don laughed.

"Yeah, okay. Her dog likes me, but doesn't like Mr. Katz. Jennifer doesn't like Mr. Katz much either, and was planning to go home and change all the locks. Do you know if he went home last night? Or did he spend the night in jail? I don't like to think of him going home and not being able to get in – I could see him breaking down a door or smashing a window."

"Mrs. Katz is perfectly safe. Mr. Katz is still in custody, but I don't think we'll be able to keep him much longer. We're having trouble tying him to either of the murders. There's just no physical evidence."

"What about the knitting needles?" Don asked.

"We got a warrant last night and tested the needles this morning. Nothing."

"So it was a waste of time."

"No. It's police work. It was a good hunch, and as a lead it made sense. It just didn't pan out.

"I still can't help thinking there's something I know that I don't know I know."

"Huh?"

I turned to Don. "I was thinking that last night. There's something niggling at the back of my brain. Something somebody said."

Petreski shook his head. "It won't come if you try to force it. You'll wake up in the middle of the night, or it'll come to you in the shower. Something like that."

"I guess."

We all sat, sipping our coffee and thinking.

"Why isn't there anything about Dawn Thrasher's murder in the news?" Don asked after a minute.

"Because…" he looked back and forth between us. "I swear to God, you tell anyone and I will never tell you anything else." We nodded. "Because her body was found in her local apartment, by police who had gone there to question her. It was kept off the scanner."

"It was you, wasn't it?" I asked. "You found her."

"Perez and, yeah, me. When she didn't answer the door we tried the knob. It was unlocked so we went in. She was in the shower; the water was still running."

"Was she stabbed? Like Wilton?"

"It looked like the same or a similar weapon, but there were multiple wounds."

"Like in *Psycho*." Don said.

"Don't be morbid, dude."

"No, I'm not. It's like in that movie, though. Someone was able to sneak up on her because she couldn't hear them, right? So it had to be someone who was watching her or knew her. Either she took a shower at the same time every day and they knew when, or they were spying on her and had some way of knowing she was in the shower –"

"Like the bathroom lights were on and the hot water heater kicked in?" I asked.

"Yeah. Or someone was there with her when she got in the shower. Someone she trusted."

"Like a lover," Petreski said.

"Or a close friend," Don said. "Jake and I do that – I'll take a shower when he's at my apartment."

"Oh?" Petreski looked at me.

"Oh, please. We've known each other for years. Get real. We're talking about Dawn Thrasher, and who she might have known well enough, or felt comfortable enough around, to take a shower while he – or she – was in her apartment."

"Whoever it was wiped the place clean. There were no prints on any doors, knobs, flat surfaces, light switches, anything. Not even Thrasher's."

"If they wiped down that much of the place," I said, "then they must have spent some time there, right? Maybe more than once, if they were concerned about fingerprints in that many places."

"That's our assumption. We're looking into as many of Dawn Thrasher's close associates as we can find. Including Josh Katz."

"That would be almost too convenient," Don said. I nodded.

"Well, gentlemen, I must be going. Thank you for the coffee. Jake, will you walk me down?"

"Huh? Oh, sure." I stood up to follow him out. Don smirked so I slapped him on the back of the head as I passed by.

Halfway down the stairs Petreski stopped and turned to me. I stepped down so I was on the step above him, even though the stairs were wide and there was room for both of us on the same step. This way I was taller.

"I'd be wasting my time if I asked you to stay out of all this." It wasn't a question.

"Yeah, probably."

"Then could the two of you at least keep it to the internet? You've actually been helpful there, and I don't want to worry about you – either of you – talking to the wrong person and putting yourselves on their radar. Okay?"

"Yeah, okay. But what if Tom Wilton's back at school tomorrow?"

"Avoid him if you can. If you can't, tell him the police found out you were talking to him and you don't want to get in trouble. Put him off. He's probably harmless – I can't see him doing this – but we don't want things getting any more complicated than they already are."

"Got it. No having lunch with other men."

"That's not what I said."

I shrugged. "Not in so many words."

"Jake…"

"Go catch the killer, Petreski. I want my real date."

Too quickly for me to react, he pulled my head down with a hand around my neck and pressed a very brief, and probably illegal, kiss to my lips. "Behave," he ordered before he turned to jog down the steps and out the door.

Don was making kissy noises when I went back to my apartment, but I took the high road and ignored him. "I'm going to call my mom," I said. "Do you want to go to Austin with me? I'm leaving Sunday and coming back Wednesday."

"I don't know. Could I bring Bridger?"

"I don't see why not, but I'll ask. If you can, do you want to?"

"Oh, man. Is it even okay if we leave town?"

"Shoot. We should have asked Petreski while he was here. Call him."

I called my mom while Don called Petreski. I figured Petreski would be glad to get us out of town for a few days.

"Jake, sweetie!"

"Hi, Mom."

"Are you still coming Sunday?"

"Well, I'm going to try. Don's finding out whether I can."

"What do you mean?"

"Well, I told you that Don and I found that body, right?"

"Oh, yes. Terrible business. But?"

"Well, Don's calling the detective in charge to find out if it's okay for us to leave town."

"Oh! But surely that's only if you're a suspect, right?"

"Yeah, but I was one for a while. And Don still might be."

"That's ridiculous."

"I know, but we found the body, so..."

"Yes, dear. I know."

Don ended his call and gave me a thumb's up.

"Don says we can leave town. Is it okay if Don comes, too?"

"Of course it is, you know that."

"And can he bring his cat?"

"His cat?"

"Remember, I told you we found that kitten?"

"Poor thing. So he decided to keep it?"

"Yeah. They're pretty inseparable. So is it okay? He's really small and he won't be any trouble."

"Yes, it's fine. We'll see you Sunday. Drive safely, dear."

"I'll do my best, Mom."

"Maybe let Don drive?"

"Mo-om!"

"I'm sorry. You know we worry."

"I'll think about," I sighed.

"Love you, dear."

"Love you, too, Mom. See you Sunday." I ended the call and turned to Don. "You and Bridger are good to go. I take it you're no longer a suspect if Petreski is letting us go."

"That's right. Funny thing, he sounded relieved when I said we were going to Austin."

"Yeah. I figured he would. Hey, do cats like riding in cars?"

"I don't think so. But he's little, maybe he'll be okay."

"You're in charge of finding out. And if he barfs in the car, you're cleaning it up."

Road Trip!

TOM WILTON was absent again on Friday, but it was the last day before Spring Break, so a lot of people were out. I couldn't tell if I should be worried or not, and it wasn't like I could call him and ask.

Don was still spending most of his time off poking around on the internet, when he wasn't training Bridger to walk on a leash. Bridger was a good little sport, and I figured they'd be taking walks around the neighborhood in no time. I could see the message boards now: "Suspicious man dragging cat around by neck" or "Urgent Alert: man using injured kitten as child bait" or something equally as paranoid.

"Just try not to get yourself shot," I told Don when we were discussing it.

"Why would I get shot?"

"Because you're going to look different. There's people like that moving into the neighborhood. Some guy pulled a gun on his neighbor when she brought over some of his mail that was left at her house by mistake."

"Did that really happen?"

"I'm just saying, I think these days some of the more dangerous people are *inside* the houses."

That got me thinking… some of the new people who were moving into those gigantic houses like Wilton was building – some of those people put up tall metal fences and pointed guns at their neighbors. And then when we were halfway to Austin I remembered what I had forgotten.

"The other day at Ground Up, when you were inside, Petreski and Perez were asking Jennifer Katz about how they got mixed up with Dawn Thrasher."

"Yeah?"

"She said some guy in the group found her online and contacted her. There was no prior connection, as far as Jennifer knew or said. She said that at first Dawn wasn't interested – not until she found out they were up against Clarence Wilton."

"So?"

"So, that's the thing that was driving me crazy. The thing I couldn't remember. We've checked out everyone *except* Wilton."

"Crap, yeah. And he's the one thing – or person – everyone's got in common. Stupid."

"What if Wilton and Thrasher had a past? We were thinking that maybe someone was obsessed with Dawn. What if it was Dawn who was obsessed with Wilton?"

"And if Dawn and Wilton had an affair, that puts Helena Wilton back at the top of the suspects list."

"Yeah," I said, drawing the word out. "But that doesn't feel right either."

"You just don't want it to be her because you like Tom and that dog."

"He seems like a nice kid. He's lonely and he got stuck with a jerk for a dad. I'd hate to think he had a killer for a mom on top of that."

We rode in silence for a while. Bridger sat up tall in Don's lap and looked out the window. He seemed to be handling riding in the car okay. We pulled into a giant travel stop with a couple dozen gas pumps and a store.

"Here," I handed Don my credit card. "Will you fill it up? I need to get some fudge and jerky for my parents."

I left Don filling up the Subaru and went inside. Mom and Dad worked hard and lived a pretty sweet life in the hills outside Austin. Mom, especially, liked getting dressed up and going to fancy parties, but she had a weakness for gas station fudge.

When I went back outside, Don had pulled the car into a parking space, but was still sitting in the driver's seat. Taking the hint, I got in on the passenger side. There was no sense making Don white-knuckle it all the way to my parents' house.

I opened the jerky and sucked on a piece as we got back on the highway.

"I thought that was for your parents."

"It's for all of us. Want a piece?"

Don shook his head.

"So, while I was in there I was thinking."

"Uh-oh."

"Helena Wilton goes to all those fancy parties and charity balls and gallery openings and stuff, right?"

"Yeah."

"The same kind of stuff my mom likes. I wonder if their paths ever crossed?"

"Would that be likely? They're in different cities."

"They are now. But maybe they met before my parents moved. And I'm going to ask my dad about Wilton. I mean, my parents aren't super rich like the Wiltons, but I could see them knowing people in common, at least. Their circles could have overlapped."

"You might as well ask."

I pulled another piece of jerky out of the package and bit off a piece.

"You know if you keep eating that the salt is going to make you all puffy and your mom is going to think you're sick."

I put the uneaten portion back in the package. I didn't need to spend the next few days with my mom making me drink nasty herbal teas.

❧

Mom didn't bother to hide the relief on her face when we pulled up and she saw Don was driving. It's no secret I'm a terrible driver, and my family doesn't let me forget it.

Mom looked the same as always – she was probably about the same age as Helena Wilton, but she looked younger. Helena showed up at the scene of her husband's death in a skirt, sweater set, and pearls, but my mom ran out to greet us in faded jeans and a thermal Henley.

"Your dad's gone to get groceries and beer – he'll be back soon. Oh! Look at this little sweetie!" Don handed Bridger to her and she got all maternal on the fuzzball. She took Don's cat and headed inside without another glance at us. We looked at each other, shrugged, and started unloading the car.

"You know you can't keep him!" I shouted as we dropped our bags in the living room.

"I don't want to keep him!" my mom hollered back from the kitchen. "But I'm going to spoil him while he's here! He's my honorary grand-kitten!" I couldn't hear the rest of what she said. It was probably baby talk for Bridger's benefit, anyway.

I rolled my eyes and Don laughed. "You and your mom are so alike."

"You take that back! I'm nothing like that wacko cat lady!"

"Your mom is awesome. Just take the compliment."

"I'm going to take a shower." I grabbed my duffle bag from the pile and headed back to the room my parents kept for me. It wasn't my childhood room – they had only moved to Austin after I started college – but it had a few of my things that my mom hadn't been able to part with and it felt like home.

I unpacked and showered, and headed back to the main part of the house and the kitchen, where I knew Mom and Don would be.

"So, dear, Don tells me you've met someone?"

I turned to glare at Don, who just blinked at me and took a bite out of the chocolate chip cookie in his hand.

"I am never, ever, bringing you here again," I told him.

"Now, Jake, don't be silly. Tell me about this boy you've met."

"He's not a boy, Mom. He's a grown up, sheesh."

"Man, then. How did you meet? What does he do?"

"You mean Don hasn't spilled all my secrets while I was out of the room?"

"Is it a secret, then?"

"I guess in a way it kind of is," I said as I pulled out a chair and took a cookie off the plate on the table. "He's a police detective, and he's working on the Wilton murder, so technically we're not supposed to – whattayacallit – fraternize."

"That sounds like a dangerous job."

"I guess so. I hadn't thought about it like that. I mean, he's always wearing fancy suits and seems… indestructible. And his partner hates me."

"She doesn't hate you."

"Don't talk with your mouth full, Don," my mom said.

"Yeah, Don. Don't talk with your mouth full." I stuck my tongue out at my best friend. My mom didn't have time to scold me, though, because the kitchen door opened and my dad came in carrying a bag of groceries.

"Hey, boys!" he greeted us. "Hi, Sweetheart," he said to my mom as she took the bag from him.

"Are there more bags, Dad?"

"Yep. Why don't you boys go get them out of the car while I start the grill?"

"I can't believe you told my mom about Petreski!" I fussed as Don and I got the groceries out of the back of my dad's station wagon.

"What was I supposed to tell her about? Your psychic visions? Your lunches with murder suspects? Your weird squirrel?"

"Raymond is not weird! You could talk about Bridger, or your job, or something."

"And when she asked for details about how we found him? And she doesn't want to hear about my job. She straight up asked me whether you were seeing anyone! I think she wants grandkids."

"Ugh. She has an honorary grand-kitten. That'll have to do her for now."

"Suck it up and deal with it."

"At least Dad got good beer."

❧

Monday morning Don and I were sprawled on lounge chairs next to my parents' pool. I had turned the heater on when I got up that morning, but the water wouldn't be warm enough for me to get in for another few hours. Don was keeping a close eye on Bridger, who was exploring my mom's herb garden. I was trying to figure out whether I could get away with drinking a beer at – I checked my phone – ten o'clock in the morning. Probably not with my mom in the house.

"Hang on – I just thought of something else," I said, putting my phone back on the table between us.

"What?"

"Last week at lunch, Tom said his parents had been arguing. About him. He said his dad had threatened to kick him out of the house when he found out he was gay, but that his mom stopped him."

"So you think maybe Tom would kill his dad to keep from getting kicked out?"

"I wasn't thinking that so much as his mom." I turned to look towards the kitchen where I could hear my mom rattling around. "My mom may seem kind of spacey and gentle if you don't really know her, but if she thought I was in danger… any kind of danger… I could see her killing someone to protect me."

"Not your *dad,* though."

"No, of course not *my* dad. But my dad's not an a-hole like Clarence Wilton was."

Things were really not looking good for Helena Wilton.

❧

"Hey, Mom?" I asked over dinner that evening. "Did you ever meet a Helena Wilton at any of those fancy parties you go to? Maybe back when you and Dad lived in Houston?"

"Hmm…" She put her fork down and picked up her wine glass. "Maybe. The name rings a bell."

"What about you, Dad? Or maybe her husband, Clarence Wilton?"

"Clarence Wilton? Isn't that the name of the man whose body you boys found?" my dad asked.

"Yeah. No one seems too broken up over him, though. Especially not his wife or son. So, I was wondering whether y'all ever met either of them. Your circles might overlap, especially when y'all were still living in Houston."

"Well, shoot," Mom said. "Now I don't know for sure whether I met her or the name sounds familiar because of this murder business. Sorry, Sweetie."

"It's okay, Mom. Maybe something will come to you later."

Dad nodded. "I'll think on it, son. I can't remember ever having any dealings with him. Maybe if I saw a picture of him it would jog my memory."

"Oh, that's an excellent idea! Do you have a picture of Helena, Jake?"

"She's all over the society pages, Mom. I'll find some pictures for you after dinner."

❧

As it turned out, neither of my parents recognized either of the Wiltons. It was a longshot, but I felt dissatisfied as we drove back to Houston.

"Even if they'd recognized them, what would that have told us?" Don asked as he merged onto the highway. I'm pretty sure Mom distracted me as we were leaving so Don could get to the car first and claim the driver's seat.

"I don't know. Maybe a new perspective from someone of the same generation? Mom's a good judge of character. If she'd said she'd met Helena and thought she seemed perfectly delightful or like a cold, brittle bitch, it would have given me a point of reference. As it is, all I know is what I see in pictures and hear from her son."

I wondered what had been going on back in Houston while we were away. Don hadn't gotten any calls, and we hadn't called Petreski – we didn't think my rambling theorizing about Helena Wilton warranted calling. Also, we hadn't had a chance to find out more about Wilton and a possible connection with Dawn Thrasher.

Tom Eavesdrops

I HAD a few more days before I needed to worry about classes again, and Don needed to make up some hours at work, so we agreed that I'd get to work on researching the Wilton/Thrasher connection.

The problem was, though, how far back did we need to go? It could have been five, ten, even twenty years ago. He could have pushed her out of his treehouse when they were kids. Should I start with the present and work my way back? Or go back as far as I could and work forwards? I knew of one person who had known Dawn when she was young, but even if he were willing to talk about her, Petreski would have a conniption fit if I tried to get information from Harry directly.

I'd start with Wilton, then. I'd make a timeline, trying to place where he was and when, then see if there was any overlap with Dawn's well-documented career.

Wilton's career was well-documented, too. And there were plenty of biographies and profiles of him online. He was a self-made man, a modern success story. Born and raised in a small town in central Texas, he had started out working construction and doing home repairs. He saved his money, moved to the city, and started flipping houses. He was smart, and ambitious, and it wasn't long before he graduated from flipping to developing.

A guy like Wilton didn't get that successful that fast without making enemies, and this wasn't telling me anything useful. I needed to look at this from a different angle – a personal angle.

I started working my way back through Dawn's career, as we knew it, to see if they were ever in the same place at the same time, or if she had ever protested any of his previous projects. I was still coming up with nothing. Wilton had never generated this much controversy before.

This was the first time Wilton had met so much resistance from a neighborhood – the first time he had tried to change the landscape of an established, largely affluent area. The Heights had been gentrifying slowly for a long time, but it had been happening organically as old residents died or moved on, and new people moved in who wanted to fix up the old houses, not tear down the Craftsman gems that gave the neighborhood its character and appeal.

Whatever had Dawn Thrasher ready to do battle against Wilton, it didn't look professional. This was looking like a personal grudge. This made things complicated, though. If Dawn had killed Wilton, then who killed Dawn? Not my problem – I'd see what I could figure out, pass it on to Petreski, and let him sort it out. Maybe give poor Hastings something to do.

I groaned and got up to move around and get something to drink. I put water on to boil and put some seeds out for Raymond. Maybe that tea Miss Nancy had blended for me would help. I should have thought of that earlier.

❧

"Let's go over what we know about Clarence Wilton."

Don groaned and sat Bridger down on the floor. "Can I at least have some coffee first?"

"Yeah, fine. There's a fresh pot in the kitchen."

Don shuffled off in that direction while I reorganized my notes for what was probably the tenth time.

"Please don't tell me you stayed up all night working on this."

"No, but I got up early. Boo came over and made me go to bed. Oh… poor Boo! What do you suppose he did while we were gone? It's not like I could leave a note on the door for him."

"He probably went to freeload at someone else's house."

"Boo's not a freeloader! And he's not like that."

"Like what?"

I shrugged. "I just can't see Boo going from house to house. He's more… deliberate… than that."

"If you say so. So what were you saying about Wilton?"

"What do we know about him?"

"You were the one doing research yesterday – you go first."

"Okay, here's the thing. He started out in a small town, built himself up from pretty much nothing. But it looks like he did it clean. Nothing anywhere that I could find indicates he ever cheated anyone or cut corners. I didn't find a whiff of workplace violations or safety issues or anything like that."

"Which means…"

"Which means, the more I look at Wilton, the more I think whoever killed him did it for personal reasons. In fact, if Dawn Thrasher hadn't wound up getting killed as well, I might be inclined to think this was a mugging gone bad or Wilton was in the wrong place at the wrong time."

Don took a sip of coffee and stared out the window.

"The thing is, though, if this is personal…" I put the thought out there.

"If it's personal, it'll be harder to figure out. We don't know who he knew, or spent time with, or talked to."

"Exactly. Maybe if I could talk to Tom…"

"Don't even think about it. Even if he wasn't a suspect – and even more so now if we're looking for a personal angle – Petreski would have kittens."

"Yeah."

"What about Thrasher?"

I shook my head. "I'm stumped."

"Well, we know Wilton didn't kill her."

"Thanks, Don. That's helpful."

"I'm thinking out loud, here. If she had some kind of connection to Wilton –"

"*Clarence* Wilton."

"Yeah. So if she had a connection to him, can we assume it got them both killed?"

"I think we have to assume their deaths are connected. It looks like the same weapon was used."

"Oh yeah. Okay." Don went into the kitchen and poured himself some more coffee.

"I think we need to focus on Dawn," I said.

"Okay. So, we know she was having an affair with Katz."

"Too specific. I mean, her personality. We know she had a habit of seducing men and using sex to manipulate them."

"Like Katz."

"Yeah, yeah, okay. Like Katz. But Katz was already sold on the save the neighborhood message. He was one of the loudest voices. So why would she seduce him?"

"Lust?"

"Have you seen Katz? No. Dawn was attractive – if she just wanted sex she could have done way better than Katz. No, she wanted something else from Katz. We just have to figure out what it was."

We sat for a few minutes drinking our coffee and staring out the windows. Raymond wasn't anywhere to be seen this morning – probably because Don was there.

"Maybe…"

"What?" Don asked.

"Okay, this is just a wild guess… but maybe Dawn wanted Clarence dead…"

"We've been thinking that."

"Yeah. But if Dawn and Clarence had a past, he would avoid her, maybe. And maybe she wasn't sure she could do it, or didn't want to do the actual deed, or whatever. So she somehow manipulated Katz into doing it."

"It's a stretch, but what about Dawn? Why would he kill her?"

"Taking his own back? Anger at her over using him? Maybe she rejected him and he snapped? That would explain why she let him into her place, why everything was wiped clean, why she would be stabbed so many times. Katz has a temper."

"I don't know…"

"Yeah. And if Dawn and Clarence had a past, we don't know about it. But his wife might."

"And that would give her a motive."

"Unless she's like Jennifer Katz and just didn't care."

"This is really making my head hurt."

❧

Tom was back in class on Monday, but he looked like hell. Petreski be damned, I made sure I met up with Tom after class.

"Hey, Tom," I called to him and waved when he stepped out of the classroom.

"Oh. Hi, Jake." He looked around before coming over to where I was standing. "I'm not sure…"

Now he was developing scruples?

"Screw it. You look like you could use a friend today. Let's go get some lunch."

He nodded, and we walked in silence to the food court.

"I was worried," I said as we sat down, "when you didn't show up for class before Spring Break."

He poked at a taco on his tray. "Yeah, I guess… I guess it finally hit me, you know? I mean, Dad was a crap dad, and a homophobe, but he was still my dad. And maybe he would have come around someday. Now…" he shrugged and poked at the taco some more.

"Now you'll never know?"

"Yeah. And to top it off… shit. I'm probably not supposed to tell you this, but you'll probably find out soon enough anyway…"

"What?"

"The police think my mom did it."

"I… I can't picture that," I said, trying to keep my voice neutral.

"It's ridiculous. Anyone who knows my mom… she's on all kinds of charity boards and does all kinds of volunteer work. She wouldn't hurt anyone!"

"Not even to protect you?"

"What do you mean?"

"I mean… don't take this the wrong way, because I'm on your side here… but maybe the police are looking at her because, well, I don't know. Did they say anything about you? Like, did they know he had threatened to kick you out? Maybe if they thought she was doing it for you? Moms will do anything for their kids."

"No! I mean, seriously, no." He shook his head.

"Okay." I didn't want to push him.

"I heard them."

That sounded promising. "Heard who?"

"The police, when they came to the house. I didn't hear everything because they were in the study and obviously they didn't let me in. But if you stand in the pantry you can hear a lot, especially if the voices are loud or deep."

"Yeah?"

"So mostly I could just hear what that one dishy detective was saying. The dark-haired one, Paretski?"

"Petreski," I said through my teeth. Tom Wilton did not need to be thinking Petreski was dishy.

"Yeah, that's the one. Anyway, I could hear him asking about some woman named Dawn."

"Dawn Thrasher?"

"I don't think that's the name they used. But it was someone else who was killed, someone he said had been linked to my dad."

"But not Thrasher?"

He shook his head. "No. I couldn't hear well."

"Wow. So did they arrest your mom?"

"No, but they searched the house. I didn't want to come to class today, but she insisted. Said I'd missed too many days already."

"That does sound like something a mom would say."

"Yeah. I think she's trying to keep it together, act like things are normal. But they're not."

"No. They definitely are not."

❧

I got a text from Don as I was walking to my car after lunch with Tom Wilton.

"*wrking happy hr 2day*"

I hated when he used numbers instead of letters, which is probably why he did it.

"*Major news! On my way.*" I messaged back. I didn't mind acronyms so much, but my phone autocorrected OMW. It made me look like an old man, but I hadn't gotten around to figuring out how to undo it. Which also made me look like an old man, now that I thought about it.

I drove straight to the restaurant where Don tended bar. Their happy hour started early, which was great for slackers, but not so great for Don, since slackers tend not to tip very well. I parked as far away as I could get from any other cars, because it's parking that's my real downfall.

When I got to the bar I slid onto a stool at one end, where I could see the rest of the bar and the restaurant entrance. One thing I had learned recently was that no matter where I went I was likely to encounter someone I knew, and I didn't necessarily want them sneaking up behind me.

Don put a beer in front of me and raised an eyebrow. I really wished I could do that. Since I couldn't, I made him wait while I took a swallow of the beer.

"Duuuude…"

"Okay, fine. I just had lunch with Tom Wilton."

"Are you kidding me?"

"No, wait. You should have seen him. He looked awful – really upset. Seems the police paid his mom a visit this morning."

"That's hardly surprising, though, is it?"

"No, but they went into the study, so he eavesdropped."

"Yeah, you two should totally be friends."

"Whatever. Tom thinks that the police think his mom did it."

"Now that is major news. Did they arrest her?"

"No, but they asked her questions about someone named Dawn, but not with the last name Thrasher."

"A married name? Or maybe a maiden name?"

"Maybe."

Don walked down the bar to serve some other slacker and I looked around. No familiar faces. Yet.

"So…?"

I turned back to Don as he approached. "Yeah," I answered. "So, it looks like Helena Wilton is now suspect number one."

"You should be glad, right? That they've got a serious suspect and this could all be coming to an end?"

"You'd think."

"But…"

"But I just can't see it."

"You just want it to be Katz."

I shrugged and took a sip of beer.

"Or is it that you just don't want it to be Tom's mother?"

"What do you mean by that?"

"I mean, for someone who's supposed to stay away from somebody, you sure do spend a lot of time with that somebody."

"That is so not what this is. You seem to have forgotten about a certain detective who's going to take me on a date as soon as this is over."

"And that scares you."

"Yeah – no! Why would that scare me?"

"Because he's a real-live grown up person. Tom is non-threatening."

"Again. That is not what this is. You are totally not getting me at all. I need to drink more beer if you're going to make a half-assed attempt at psychoanalyzing me."

Don shrugged and I drank some more beer. I was pissed off, not just because he was wrong, but because not so long ago he wouldn't have been wrong. There was a time when I had avoided serious relationships, or any kind of relationship. But it was a phase – part of growing up – and I had worked it out of my system. Don, though… Don had always been a commitment kind of guy.

"Okay," I said, putting down my half-finished beer. "My turn."

"Huh?"

"I know what's eating you."

"Oh yeah?" His eyebrow went up again, the show-off.

"Yeah. You're pissed off because you're the one who's always been the romance and flowers and finding 'the one' guy. I've always been the… the… bumble-bee floating around the garden and never settling down. And now I've found somebody who might be the real deal, and you're… ohmigod – you're jealous!"

"I'm not." He looked down and started wiping the bar with the towel he'd had tossed over his shoulder.

"Don."

He ignored me, not looking up.

"Don. Donny. DonnyDonnyDonDon."

"Stop it, dude." He sounded pissed off, but I could see his lips quirk.

I leaned as far over the bar as I could to get up in his face.

"Don, just because I've met Mr. Right doesn't mean there's not someone out there for you. I mean, seriously, we're not even fishing in the same pond, you know?"

He shrugged.

"It happens when it happens. Your someone is probably so special and awesome and kickass that you're not ready yet, so fate is making you wait until you can see her and not spontaneously combust."

"Jake. Seriously, I am begging you. Stop reading paranormal romance."

"Just wait. You'll see."

Jake is Not Convinced

I WAS having a chat with Raymond the next morning, trying to decide whether meditation was something I should try. My mom and Miss Nancy would probably say yes. Don would roll his eyes. Raymond cocked his head and I picked up some calm vibes that I took to mean that he was on board with the meditation plan.

"I think so, too, Ray," I said. "I mean, with all the crazy that's been going on around me lately, maybe it would help me focus and prioritize. And I could get one of those cool cushions to sit on."

I took a sip of my coffee and thought about how having chats with a squirrel named Raymond was probably going to be part of my new normal. I could live with that.

A knock at the door sent Raymond skittering back up the tree and I got up to let Don in.

"Am I interrupting?" He asked. "I thought I heard voices."

"I was just discussing the merits of meditation with Raymond. What's up?"

"You were… no. Not asking. What's up is more important. Have you looked at the news this morning?"

"No. What happened?"

I moved to the coffee table and opened my laptop.

"Helena Wilton was arrested early this morning."

"No!"

I opened one of the local news websites and there it was, with video and pictures and everything: "Local Philanthropist Arrested for Developer Husband's Murder".

"Holy crap," I whispered.

"Yeah."

"Look how calm she looks."

The video showed Helena Wilton, in handcuffs, being escorted from her River Oaks mansion to an unmarked police car. Detective Perez, her face grim, was at Helena's side. Helena's face was unreadable, her hair in a twist and her make-up perfect. She'd probably take a glamourous mugshot. I didn't see Petreski anywhere.

"They must have found out something new," Don said. "Some new evidence."

"Hmm."

"Let me guess. You're not buying it."

"I'm not ruling it out completely. I'd like to know what they found that was big enough to arrest her for, though."

"Maybe it's in the article." Don started scrolling down, reading the text below the video. "Ugh, don't they have proofreaders look at this stuff before they post it?"

"Oh man. I wonder how Tom is handling this?"

"You couldn't call him, even if you had his number. Do you have his number?"

"No, I don't."

Don's phone rang and we both turned to look at it where it sat on the coffee table.

"Do *you* have his number?" I asked.

"Don't be ridiculous. I've never even spoken to him. Oh, it's Petreski."

"Answer it! Answer it!"

"I am. Geez. Hello? Yes, we saw it on the news. He's right here." He handed the phone to me.

"Hello?"

"Jake, Don said y'all saw Helena Wilton's arrest on the news."

"Yeah. She didn't look like she was worried. I don't think she did it."

"People with as much money and as many lawyers as she has don't worry."

"Wow. Cynical."

I could practically hear him shrug. "You see it happen."

"Or… and here's a thought… she's not worried because she didn't do it. That's my bet."

"Your money's still on Katz?"

"Yeah."

"There's just no evidence, Jake."

"He and Jennifer were arguing about something major the night Dawn Thrasher was killed. Or whatever her name was."

"What?"

"What what?"

"Dawn whatever her name was? What do you mean?"

"I mean, her name wasn't always Thrasher, right? And whatever else her name was, I'm guessing it connected her to the Wiltons somehow."

He was silent, and I waited.

After a few moments he sighed, and I sat back on the sofa, the phone pressed to my ear.

"No, it wasn't. What do you know? You need to tell me."

"Only that someone heard you refer to her by a name other than Thrasher. I don't know what, though."

More silence.

"Wilton."

"What?"

"Dawn Thrasher was born Dawn Wilton. She was the daughter of Clarence's older brother, Roger."

"She was Clarence's niece?" Don turned to look at me when I said that, and I nodded at the shocked look on his face.

"Yes. And now I've told you more than I should. I need to go."

"Wait – why did you call in the first place?"

"What?"

"Why did you call?"

"Just, uh, checking in. Making sure you and Don were doing okay. No more threats or uncomfortable encounters, that kind of thing? Right. Okay, gotta go."

The line went silent and I looked at the phone before handing it back to Don.

"So weird." I said.

"What?"

"He called us for, like, no reason."

"Did he?"

"Yeah."

"Or did he call to tell you something?"

"Tell me what? I had to pick information out of him."

"But he told you, didn't he? I mean, maybe he called so you could ask him the right questions. Maybe he doesn't think it's Helena either, but he's got no choice but to arrest her at this point."

"You mean, he was being devious? That is so him."

"And he knew that if he gave us the information we wanted – that he wanted us to have – that we would keep poking at it."

"That is so us," I agreed.

"It is."

"So let's poke."

"Ew. Dude."

"Okay, that sounded bad. But you know what I mean."

"So bad. I'm telling Petreski you wanted to poke me."

"I am so killing you. Bridger will be an orphan and it will be your fault."

"Jake." Don turned to me, his face serious. "If anything ever happens to me, you have to promise to take care of Bridger."

"What the fuck, dude? I mean, yeah, of course. But… oh. Ha ha ha. Very funny. You really should consider a career on the stage. Maybe that's what the road opener candle is trying to tell you."

❧

Back we went to the digital drawing board, searching for any information we could find on Roger Wilton and his family. We found a record of his marriage to Amelia Thrasher in 1962, and the birth of a daughter, Dawn, in 1967. Dawn must have taken her mother's maiden name at some point – but when, and why?

Roger was killed in an automobile accident in 1979. The obituary scanned from a local newspaper didn't give much information, just listing his survivors and information about the services. Dawn would have been twelve. Clarence would have been twenty, just getting started on his handyman/builder career.

I was trying to figure out how any of this would have fit together. We had no way of knowing the Wilton family dynamics. Were they close? Did the accident make them rally together and take care of each other? Or did it drive them apart?

My money was on the latter, since Dawn Wilton became Dawn Thrasher. I wondered whether her mother was still alive, and where. Had she gone back to her maiden name? Petreski probably had some of the answers, but couldn't tell us. Or maybe he didn't. Maybe Hastings was phenomenally bad at his job.

Don, though… Don had Google-Fu like nobody's business.

"Don?"

"Hmm?" He didn't look up from his laptop.

"Don, I think I know what the road opener candle is trying to tell you."

"Oh yeah? What's that?"

"I think you should be doing Hastings's job. You know, information analyst stuff like Hastings is supposed to be doing. Look at what you've found just in the public records. Imagine what you could do if you had access to the private stuff."

Don looked up at that, then off into the distance. He was thinking about it. "Maybe."

"I could totally see you doing that."

"Yeah. But first, let's figure this out. Life plans can wait until tomorrow."

"Do you think Amelia's still alive?"

"I'm trying to figure that out. I'm looking for death records or obituaries, but I haven't found anything yet for either name."

"She could have gotten remarried, and have a completely different name now."

"But then her marriage record should show up, and I'm not finding anything like that, either."

"If she is alive, and the police know that Dawn Thrasher was born Dawn Wilton, then they should know about Amelia also, right? If she is still alive, they would have notified her of her daughter's death."

"Makes sense."

I looked back at the screen, at the minimalist obituary for Roger Wilton, and wondered why it was so sparse. "I wish we knew more about the accident that killed Roger."

"Why? You think there was something hinky about it?"

"I think… I think *something's* hinky. It was a small town, and small towns put *everything* in the paper. There should be an article about the crash, right?"

"Yeah. But it looks like the paper isn't all online. They probably have all the back issues in an archive."

"Is the paper still in business?"

"It publishes weekly now, but yeah. We could call them, see what they have?"

"I was thinking road trip."

"Road trip? But if we call they can just send us a copy of the pertinent article."

"But what if something else is pertinent? What if there's something else in the paper that can put it in perspective?"

"You're just bored and want to take a road trip."

"Are you working today?"

"No." Don's shoulders slumped.

"Road trip! And Bridger stays here – they won't let him in the newspaper archive."

"Fine."

A Day in the Country

WE PULLED into Mesquite Springs in time for a late lunch at a diner on the main strip. All the locals turned to look at us as we sat at the counter. Don looked around while I charmed the waitress. Middle-aged ladies love me – I bring out their maternal instincts.

"Everybody's staring at us, dude," Don whispered after he placed his order.

"Well, yeah. We don't live here, so they're curious."

"It feels weird."

"Imagine how weird it would be if you were wearing a sling with a cat in it."

"Point."

"Whatchew two boys up to, then?" a deep voice asked from somewhere over my left shoulder.

I turned to see a table of three older men, two wearing VFW caps and the third, the one who had spoken, tilting his chair back on two legs to look up at me where I sat on the bar stool.

"Chuck Ferris!" the waitress fussed as she passed behind him. "How many times have I told you not to do that? You're gonna bust another chair!"

The chair dropped to the floor, but the man never took his eyes off us.

"Well, sir. We're in town to do a little research at the newspaper, but we've been on the road for a while and wanted a bite of lunch first."

"Research? What kind of research?"

"Well, I understand Clarence Wilton grew up here. We're working on a profile of him, how he got his career started, that kind of thing."

"Clarence Wilton?" one of the VFW caps said. "Ain't he the one got himself murdered down in Houston?"

"Yes, sir. That's right."

"Why'd you wanna do a profile about him?"

"Well, he was very successful. Built his business up from nothing. People could learn from that kind of entrepreneurship."

One of the VFW caps snorted.

"You a reporter or somethin'?" Chuck asked.

"A student."

"Ain't you a little old to be a student?" the second VFW cap asked.

"Well, I admit it's taking me longer than it should."

Chuck stood and pulled his wallet out of his back pocket. "I gotta get goin'. Bill, Gary, see y'all tomorrow."

No one spoke as Chuck went to the register, paid his bill, and left.

Bill and Gary turned to look at us, and I realized we were alone in the diner with them, the waitress, and whoever was in the kitchen.

"Y'all from Houston, then?" one of them asked.

"Yes, sir."

"Don't know how much you'll find out about Clarence Wilton, to be honest." He shook his head. I wasn't necessarily looking for information about Clarence, so that was okay.

"Well, we have to start somewhere, right? I don't suppose either of y'all knew him or remember him from back then?"

They looked at each other, and shrugged. "A bit. He wasn't such a nice boy. I don't imagine he was all that nice grown up, neither."

"That's the impression I'm starting to get."

"Left town, and that's the last this town heard of him. Never came back, family never heard from him. Nothin'."

"Is there any of his family still around?"

The old man tilted his head back, looking at the ceiling, and it reminded me of Miss Nancy's thinking face. "Not that I can think of. You, Bill?"

Bill shook his head. "Nope."

"Nope," Gary repeated. "Parents died years ago. Brother, too. Just the brother's girl and her ma left, but they left town after the brother got killed and never came back."

"You don't happen to know where she – the brother's wife, that is, went, do you?"

"Amelia, her name was. Heard she met a feller and moved off with him. Oklahoma or someplace Never heard nothin' after that."

I heard the waitress put our plates on the counter behind me, and Bill and Gary got up to leave. As Bill made his way to the register, Gary came over to stand next to us at the counter.

"So, Houston, huh?"

"Yes, sir." I nodded.

"I hear y'all got a place there called Montrose. Where the queer folks can hang out and be queer without nobody givin' a damn. Is that right?"

"Well, yes. Pretty much."

"Hmm." He looked over to where Bill was paying their check, and Bill rolled his eyes. "They got any bars there that cater to the, uh, older crowd? Like say, if a couple wanted to, uh, swing a bit? Or, uh, meet someone to, uh, spend some time with. Still as a couple, mind."

"Uh… probably. I think that's probably something that… uh… someone could find."

Gary nodded and moved on to catch up with his, uh, fellow veteran.

"I think I've lost my appetite," Don said, looking down at the BLT on his plate.

"I… uh…"

The waitress chuckled as she passed by. "Better find it, boys, or you don't get no pie!"

"You're not my real mom!" I called out to her, and she laughed harder.

Don ate a potato chip and I choked down a bite of mashed potatoes. Gary and Bill were pretty spry, and not bad-looking for old guys, but I was trying to eat, here.

I was halfway through my chicken-fried steak when the waitress came back to refill my tea.

"You're lucky you weren't in here on your own," she told me.

"Why's that?"

"You're just their type, honey. If you'd given 'em half a chance they'd've had you hogtied and –"

"Oh. My. God. Please stop talking! This is, like, a small town! Aren't you supposed to be lecturing me on the evil of my ways and damning Bill and Gary to hell or something?"

"Pfft. Gary was Chief of Police for over twenty years. Bill was president of the savings and loan. If you wanted to buy a house or stay out of jail, you learned to keep your mouth shut. Once folks saw how Gary and Bill took care of this town, and each other, most of 'em just got on with their lives and didn't give it any thought."

"Wow," Don breathed, and took a bite of his sandwich.

"Yeah, but I still don't want to be… or think about being… you know. Ack."

She chuckled. "Tell you what. You boys finish your lunches and you get pie on the house."

&

After lunch we walked the two blocks to the newspaper office. I was feeling uncomfortably full, but Don had gone with a lighter lunch and the lemon icebox pie, so he was doing fine. I, on the other hand, was determined to have pie and ate an entire twelve-ounce chicken-fried steak, mashed potatoes with gravy, fried okra, and a biscuit. I topped this carbo-feast off with a slice of pecan pie, and now I was having regrets.

"We'll have a light dinner," Don said.

"I'm not eating again for at least two days."

"You can go for a walk tomorrow."

"Urg."

"You have a food baby," he said, poking my belly.

"Ow! Mean!"

"Unbutton your jeans if you're that uncomfortable."

"I couldn't. That would be tacky!"

"And eating that entire steak, plus that monster slice of pie, wasn't tacky?"

"I couldn't insult the cook."

Don shook his head. Obviously he couldn't argue with my logic.

The *Mesquite Springs Weekly* (formerly the *Mesquite Springs Daily*) was housed in a red brick building just two blocks from the diner. Mesquite Springs wasn't the county seat, so there was no courthouse square. There was a central business district, though, which included the diner, bank, library, town offices, a grocery store, a feed store, and various other businesses and shops. I had seen a couple of bed and breakfasts on side streets, and signs for wineries on the way into town. It looked like Mesquite Springs was gearing up to market itself as a wine-lover's destination.

The newspaper office was quiet. I could hear someone tapping away at a keyboard somewhere, but the only person I could see was a middle-aged woman in jeans and a Garth Brooks concert t-shirt who stood and came to meet us at the tall front desk.

"You boys aren't from around here," she observed in a deep west-Texas twang.

"I guess that makes three of us, then," I said and felt Don's pointy elbow jabbing my ribs. "Ow!"

She studied us over the top of her glasses for few seconds before grinning. "Whadda y'all need? An ad or somethin'?"

"We were hoping to do some research in the archives?"

She reached under the counter and pulled out a key on a bright orange lanyard.

"Sure. Follow me." She led us around the counter and down a hallway before stopping in front of a closed door with a plate reading "Archive" mounted at eye level.

"Okay, boys. House rules."

We nodded.

"No food, no drink, no chewing gum, not even a breath mint. No scissors, no knives, no rippin' or tearin'. Got it?"

"Yes, ma'am." We both answered.

"If you want somethin' copied, mark it with one of the paper slips in the box on the table, and we'll copy everything at one time before you leave. Copies are fifty cents each. Don't put the books back on the shelves yourselves. Leave 'em on the table and we'll shelve them later." She paused and we nodded.

"Your hands clean?"

We nodded again.

"You need a bathroom break, it's at the end of this hallway on the left. Books are in chronological order, starting to the right of the door when you get inside. You got any questions, come back out front and one of us can help you. If you do run across anything that's missing or torn or messed up, I'd appreciate it if you'd mark it and let us know. Okay?

"Yes, we will," I nodded and she unlocked the door.

I'd never used a newspaper archive before, but I'd seen a few episodes of *History Detectives*, and given her list of rules I was surprised she hadn't handed us gloves before letting us in. The archive room was larger than I expected, and I discovered why when I looked at the date for the first bound volume: July 23, 1900. That was almost one hundred years of daily papers, and weekly since 1999.

"That is a *lot* of papers." Don turned around in a circle, his eyes scanning the shelves.

"Yeah," I said. "Good thing we have a date."

I put my backpack on the long table in the middle of the room and took out my laptop. While I waited for it to boot up I found the volume containing the date of Roger's death in 1979. Don took the volume after it, and we started searching for any mention of the accident specifically, or the Wiltons or Thrashers in general.

"Have you ever looked at really old newspapers?" Don asked after a few minutes.

"How old are we talking about?"

"I remember looking at a small town paper from, like, the 1920s or something like that. Anyway, they printed *everything*. A stranger couldn't come to town without it being in the paper. If someone's cousin came to visit, or someone took a trip or, well, just about anything, it was in the announcements in the paper."

"Too bad they weren't still doing that in 1979."

"Yeah."

I found the obituary right away, and started working backwards to see if I could find out more about the accident, or about Roger, Clarence, or anyone or anything related. I had no idea what I was looking for – anything that would give me some clue about the families and why Dawn Wilton became Dawn Thrasher.

&

We had each finished the volumes we started with and moved on to the next when I decided I needed a break. I found the bathroom down the hall, then wandered back out to the front office.

"Need anything, hon?" the lady in the Garth shirt asked.

"No, ma'am, just wanted to stretch my legs a little."

She nodded and turned her attention back to the monitor in front of her. I moved to stand at the door and looked out the window at the quiet street in front of me.

"What're y'all lookin' for in there?"

I turned to see an older man, about the same age as Bill and Gary back at the diner, leaning on the counter. I guessed he was probably the one I had heard typing when we came in.

"Just doing some research for school. On Clarence Wilton." I stuck with the story I'd used at the diner.

"Now that's a name I haven't heard in a long time. Until last week, of course. Bad business, that. You a journalism student, then? Writing a story about him?"

"No. Business, actually. Entrepreneurship. We're doing a profile on his business, how he built it up from scratch and became so successful. That kind of thing. He started out here, so…" I shrugged.

"Sure, sure." The man nodded. "Makes sense."

"I don't suppose you knew him back then?"

"A little. Knew his brother better. Roger." The man shook his head. "Sad business."

Now, this sounded promising.

"I think I saw something in the paper. He was killed, right? A car accident?"

"Well… that's what they finally decided."

"But you didn't think so?"

"No one really thought so, but nobody could ever prove anything different. The police – well, I don't think they tried very hard. Didn't want the mess. Back then – before Gary came back and cleaned up the department – certain folks could get away with things."

I nodded.

"But I shouldn't be filling your head with old rumors and gossip."

"Well, anything that could help me build a picture of the man would be a help. I don't suppose there's any family left?"

"Oh, long gone. The parents died a while back. After Roger died, his widow tried to make a go of it here, but with no money and Roger's family not helping any, she finally left. Headed off to Oklahoma, I heard."

"No money? Wasn't there any insurance or anything?"

"Now, that's what had everybody talking. Roger, bless his soul, loved his wife and daughter to pieces, but he was a procrastinator and a bit absentminded. Seems he never got around to changing the beneficiary on his life insurance."

I had a feeling I knew where this was going.

"So when he got killed, all that money – half-a-million dollars – went to his baby brother."

"And that's where Clarence really got the money to get his business off the ground," I said.

"Yep. Caused a real scandal. Folks tried to reason with him, but he had big plans for himself and that money. The local clergy even went to see him, tried to appeal to his Christian nature. Fat lot of good that did."

"And his parents?"

"Let's just say the apple that was Clarence didn't fall far from the tree. Those two never cared about anyone but themselves. It wasn't a surprise to anyone when Clarence left town and never looked back. Every man for himself in that family. That the kind of thing you're lookin' to find out?"

"In a way," I said, remembering my cover story. "I don't think running off with half-a-mil in insurance money at the expense of widows and children really qualifies as entrepreneurship."

"Nope. I guess not. Sorry about that."

"No. It's good I found out before we turned in that paper, you know? I'd better go tell my friend. Thanks. Thanks a lot."

❧

"So let me get this straight," Don said as we drove back to Houston. "Clarence got the insurance money that really should have been for Dawn and her mother, leaving them high and dry?"

"Yep."

"And most everybody in town figured there was something shady about the accident."

"Yep."

"But the police couldn't prove anything."

"I don't think they really tried. I got the impression that maybe the local police were either bought off or turned a blind eye."

"Well, if Dawn blamed Clarence for her father's death, or keeping the money that should have gone to her mother, that would definitely be a motive. But what about means and opportunity? You've gotta have all three."

"If Dawn manipulated Josh Katz into doing it, he would be the one who'd have to have the means and opportunity. Maybe he took the dog for a walk, knowing Wilton would be doing the same."

"Maybe. Wouldn't his wife wonder, though, if he took the dog for a walk at an odd time?"

"Maybe it wasn't an odd time. Maybe it was the normal time, and he knew where Wilton would be because he'd seen him there before."

"Which brings up something that's been bothering me since Helena was arrested."

"What's that?" I asked.

"If Wilton lived in River Oaks, what was he doing walking his dog in Woodland Heights that late at night?"

Jake Visits Tom's Love Nest

OF COURSE we called Petreski and told him everything we'd learned. Because we're fine, upstanding citizens, right? Hearing the sound of his voice was just an added bonus, I swear.

Don mentioned the disconnect between Wilton living in River Oaks, but walking his dog in Woodland Heights late at night. Petreski didn't have an answer for that, and didn't sound too thrilled when I suggested that maybe Tom would know.

"I know that look," Don said after we ended the call. "You're going to talk to Tom Wilton, aren't you?"

"If he knows why his dad would have been there, it might tell us something."

"Are you *trying* to piss Petreski off?"

"No. I just can't help thinking that the police are missing something important. They've got the wrong person locked up."

"Are you sure, though? Wouldn't Helena have known her husband's habits? She would have known where to find him."

"Not necessarily. Haven't we pretty much determined they lived separate lives?"

"Geez. Fine, but try not to get in trouble or stir stuff up, okay? Petreski already sounded annoyed."

"I'll bet he's annoyed because they can't find any evidence that Helena did it."

"They wouldn't have arrested her in the first place if they didn't have something."

I shook my head. "I need to talk to Tom. And maybe Miss Nancy."

❧

Tom missed class again, but I wasn't surprised. One parent dead, the other arrested for murder – I'd stay home, too.

I knew I shouldn't, but I looked up Tom's email address in the student directory and sent him a message. Nothing big, just "Hey, are you okay? Do you need notes from class?"

The reply came within five minutes. "I am totally not okay. Call me? 832-555-4718."

This was what I'd wanted, right? I knew Petreski would be pissed off, but I had to make this call. Tom answered before the first ring finished.

"Hello?"

"Hey. It's Jake. How you holding up, man?"

"Seriously shitty. Mom is still in jail and I swear, there is no way she would have done this. No way."

"I believe you."

"You do? You're the only one, I bet."

"Your mom does a lot of good for people. I'll bet they don't believe it, either."

I could hear him sigh, but he didn't say anything else.

"You need anything? I can send you notes from class."

"Can you come over?"

"I don't know…"

"Please? Right now, it's like, you're the only friend I've got. You're the only one who's not judging me or Mom."

I could hear Petreski's voice in my head. "Whatever you do, don't go over to Tom Wilton's love nest."

"Sure. What's the address?"

❧

I followed Tom's directions and parked in the circular drive in front of the mansion I had seen on the news. There were no vans or reporters to be seen today, though. I walked around to the back of the rambling house and knocked on the door Tom had indicated.

I looked around – it was a sweet set-up with its own small patio and a path that led to a break in a hedge. Through the gap I caught a glimpse of a larger patio and a swimming pool.

I heard the door open and turned to see Tom in the doorway, looking tired, but at least he was clean.

"Just get out of the shower?" I asked, pointing to his wet hair.

"Yeah. After I got off the phone with you I realized I hadn't had a shower in, like, three days. I was unfit for human company. Sorry, come on in." He stepped back so I could enter.

I wasn't sure what I had expected, but the place looked like his mom had probably decorated it. The furniture all matched. There were coordinating pillows on the sofas and actual paintings on the walls. It didn't look like a college student's apartment. Turn the lights down low, light a few candles, and voilà – love nest.

"Have a seat. Want anything to drink? I've got beer, wine, coke?"

"Dr. Pepper?"

"Yeah. Be right back."

I sat on one of the grey sofas and looked around. I could hear Tom in the kitchen, and after a minute I felt something brush against my leg. I looked down to see Murphy sniffing my feet.

"Hey, Murphy," I whispered. "Remember me?"

He looked up and wagged his tail as I stroked his back. I scratched his side and the tail moved faster, his whole body getting in on the act.

"Looks like you found his sweet spot," Tom said, setting a tray on the coffee table in front of me. He had poured my drink into a glass with ice – fancy, but I figured he was used to the finer things. He picked up his own drink – a glass of white wine – and sat back in the sofa, slightly turned to face me.

"Yeah, well dogs are pretty easy. They've all got one and it's not usually hard to find."

Tom sipped his wine and I looked back down at Murphy.

"How's he been doing? Still upset?"

"He seems better. He's quite the escape artist, though. I was going to put in a dog door, but he can't be trusted."

"Escape artist?"

"Yeah. Dad always… Dad always used to say he should have named him Houdini. Now I know what he meant."

"So he gets out a lot?" That would explain why sometimes I dreamed about running loose and hunting. Murphy the escape artist. "You're a real troublemaker, aren't you?" I asked, looking down at the dog, who had rolled onto his back so I could rub his belly.

Tom snorted. "Yeah. But I don't know… he seems okay, but when he gets out he heads for the bayou. I wonder if maybe he's looking for Dad."

"Your dad always walked him there? In The Heights?"

"Not always. But after he decided to start buying property there, he would go over there all the time. He'd walk along the bayou and the esplanades. He said it was to get a feel for the place, but that was bullshit."

Something in his tone made me look back up at him. The wine glass was almost empty. He looked down into it, then got up and headed for the kitchen. He was back a minute later with the bottle, filling his glass and setting the bottle on the table.

"What did you mean?" I asked.

"Hmm?"

"About getting a feel for the place being bullshit?"

"Oh. Dad did whatever he wanted, right? He always had a plan, and getting a feel for a place? He'd never cared about that before. I don't know… maybe he was having a mid-life crisis or something." He shrugged and sipped his wine. Maybe this was going to be one of those questions that couldn't be answered. Who could really know what went on in another person's mind? In the end it didn't matter *why* Clarence Wilton walked his dog where he did. What mattered was that someone knew and took advantage of that fact.

I picked up my own drink, and looked at it for a few seconds before putting it back down. I remembered Petreski's warning again. I didn't think Tom would have put anything in it, but I wasn't taking any chances.

In a flash of clarity I realized that coming here was a mistake. Anything I'd get from Tom would be speculation, and coming here might have given him the wrong idea. I needed to get out of there.

"Something wrong with your drink?" Tom asked.

"No. It's fine."

"I've got other choices. Iced tea. I can get another glass if you'd like some wine?"

"No, thanks. It just suddenly hit me that I probably shouldn't be here, you know? I mean, it's fine at school and all, but this might look suspicious."

Tom shrugged again. "I'm kind of beyond caring at this point."

"You shouldn't be. You should care a whole damn lot. It's your mom who's in jail."

He flinched at that and I felt bad, but if he needed a friend right now, he needed the kind of friend who would tell him the hard, unvarnished truth.

"Tom?" I took the wine glass from his hand and set it on the table. "Tom, I need you to listen to me, okay?"

He looked up and met my eyes. I could tell he was trying not to cry, and was impressed he hadn't given in yet. I would have. He nodded.

"I really, honestly, do believe that your mom didn't do this, okay?"

"Okay."

"But there are a lot of people – mainly the police – who think she did. And they are the ones who matter."

He nodded.

"Right. So you need to put down the wine, take care of yourself, and get your act together so you can be strong for her. She needs people on her side who believe in her. You need to stick up for her like she stuck up for you."

He nodded again, his lip trembling.

"So, I'm going to get out of here, okay? Because we really aren't supposed to be hanging out."

He stood and squared his shoulders. "Yeah. Yeah, you're right. Maybe… maybe after this is all over we could get together?"

I stood and stepped around the coffee table towards the door.

"I'd like that, Tom, if you mean as friends, right?"

He looked confused and kind of cute, and I had to admit that he wasn't unattractive. "Sorry, I thought…"

"I'm… I'm kind of seeing someone. I'm sorry if I gave you the wrong impression."

"No, it's cool. Really. Thanks for… well… thanks for being a friend. Does that sound lame?"

"No. Not at all. Hang in there, and if you really need me, call. Okay?"

He nodded and I let myself out.

There was someone leaning against my car when I came around the side of the house, and I cringed when I realized it was Petreski. I was about to get an earful. One look at Petreski's face and I wondered whether I might be free to take Tom up on his offer after all.

"So, heya, Detective Petreski."

He didn't say anything, but his glare was damn eloquent.

"What, uh, brings you out to this neck of the woods?"

More silent glaring. He was an excellent glarer, I had to admit.

"I was, uh, going to call you…"

"Is that so?" Apparently he could talk and glare at the same time.

"Yeah. I, um, well…"

"You decided to visit Tom Wilton, son of the murder victim *you found*, and son of his accused murderer, and you didn't think maybe you should call me *first*?"

"You forgot cousin of the other victim."

"What?!" His nostrils flared.

"Nothing. Never mind."

"People are *dying*, Jake. There is a… a… really bad energy around this family, for lack of a better word. You need to be staying away from them, not visiting them in their *homes*. Homes, by the way, that I specifically told you to stay away from."

Told me to stay away from? I was fine with being scolded, because I figured I deserved it and I knew he was worried about me, but he did not get to *tell* me what I could and could not do. I think he realized his mistake right after he said it, because he shut up real fast as I drew myself up and straightened my shoulders.

"How did you know I was here?"

"What?"

"Are you following me?"

"No! Of course not. We have the house staked out. If anyone leaves or comes calling, Perez and I get a call. When I realized you were here, I came."

"Because I was visiting Tom Wilton's 'love nest'?"

"Um –"

"He's my friend now, like it or not. And he needed a friend. His dad is dead, and his mom is in jail, yeah. So – surprise – he's feeling kinda down and needed someone to talk to. Get over it."

"I –"

"Oh, and yes, he asked me out. I turned him down, but the offer is probably still on the table."

"Jake –"

"What?" I'm pretty sure I suck at glaring, but I was giving it my best shot.

"Look. I'm sorry. I've got a job to do here and I could have phrased that better –"

"You could have *phrased* it better?"

"What?" He looked confused and pissed off.

"You think *that* would solve the problem? If you had *phrased it better*?"

"I'm trying to keep you safe!"

"Then go catch the real murderer!"

I stepped past him, dodging out of the way when he reached for my arm, and got into my car. I could hear him calling my name, and as I pulled away I looked in the rearview mirror to see him as he watched me leave, hands on his hips and mouth drawn into an angry frown. It would have been a picture perfect exit if I hadn't mistimed my turn and hopped the curb as I left.

A Visit Goes Awry

I DROVE towards home, trying to concentrate on what I was doing and not on how angry I was. Or how scared – because if I pissed him off too much, Petreski might not come back. But even so, he did not get to order me around. I thought I had made that perfectly clear.

I was restless, and not ready to go home, where I'd probably have to tell the whole sad story to Don and listen to him tell me he told me so. So, with Helena Wilton in jail – and Josh Katz probably out – I decided to go check on Jennifer Katz. Maybe her husband wasn't a murderer after all – again, not convinced – but he was still a cheating scumbag and she could probably use a friend. I was hardly snooping at all.

It wasn't hard to find the Katzes' address, since they were so active in the neighborhood. The house was a two-story four-square with a large covered porch. Someone in the family had a green thumb – the flower beds were full of bushes and fresh plantings getting ready to bloom. Blue-glazed flower pots overflowed with bright pink geraniums on either side of the porch steps. I couldn't picture Josh working in the garden, so this must have been Jennifer's work.

I rang the doorbell and stepped back from the door. I could hear Buttercup barking, and footsteps approaching. Mrs. Katz's face appeared in the small window in the door and she smiled before opening it.

"Hello, Jake! How are you? What brings you by?"

"I just wanted to check on you and Buttercup. See how you were doing."

"Oh, that's so sweet. Come on in." She held the door open and I stepped inside. The blinds were all open and sunlight streamed in.

"This is really nice," I said.

"Thanks. I'm going to redecorate. Paint it a more cheerful color. Fresh start, you know?"

"Sounds like a good idea."

"Would you like a gin and tonic?" she asked.

I was more of a beer drinker, but since it wasn't likely she had beer in the house, I decided to join her. "Sure, why not?"

I followed her into the kitchen where a bottle of gin already sat on the counter. She went to the pantry and came back with a fresh bottle of tonic water. "Josh hates gin. Now that he's gone, I'm going to try them all. Especially the expensive ones."

"Sounds, um, interesting."

She laughed. "Don't worry. I'm not going off on a bender or anything. I'm just not going to let anyone stop me from doing what I really want from now on." She took a couple of glasses from a cabinet, setting them on the counter before opening the freezer. "Oh, bother. The freezer must be on the blink again. The ice is all stuck together."

She opened a drawer and started rummaging around. "That's odd. I could have sworn it was in here." She moved to the next drawer and started shifting the contents around.

"What are you looking for?" I asked.

"The ice pick. The ice in the freezer is always sticking together, and it should be in here."

I pulled open the first drawer. "Maybe you just overlooked it. What does it look like?"

"Nothing fancy. Wooden handle, and a metal spike about," she held her fingers a few inches apart, "so long."

I froze. "When… when was the last time you saw it?"

"Oh, it's been a while. Maybe three or four weeks since the last time we used it." She was still rummaging. She hadn't made the connection yet.

"Mrs. Katz…"

"Jennifer." She turned to smile at me. "I'll never be Mrs. Katz again as…" her voice trailed off and her eyes got wide.

"What?" I thought I knew what.

"The…" she looked down at the open drawer. "The ice pick's not here, is it?"

"I have a really bad feeling it isn't. Has anyone other than you or Mr. Katz been in the house recently?"

"As far as I know just the police, when they came for my needles. No… wait… Josh hosted a meeting here one evening. The protest group. I wasn't here, though. I was teaching a knitting class up in Spring. I didn't get home until the meeting was over. I don't know who was here."

I heard a slapping, banging sound from the next room and jumped.

"It's okay," Jennifer said. "It's just Buttercup using the pet door."

I started backing out of the kitchen, towards the front door, motioning for Jennifer to follow me. "Okay, sure." But I felt uneasy about that sound, and I could have sworn I'd seen Buttercup in the living room not five minutes earlier. Quick and stealthy, Buttercup was not.

"So, what color were you thinking about painting in here?" I asked, still moving towards the door. Jennifer followed, eyes fixed on my face.

"Oh," she glanced down to where Buttercup stretched out on his bed in front of the fireplace. I had to hand it to her, she kept her head and her voice stayed steady. I suppose living with a human powder-keg for years could give a person nerves of steel. "Oh, I've always loved the ocean. I was thinking of something tropical. Like aqua, maybe?"

"Sounds great." I felt the door at my back and reached behind me to open it. "What about the furniture?" I asked as I turned the knob.

"Oh, all new, probably."

I got the door opened and pushed her through it just as Josh Katz charged through the dining room door, ice pick held high. He came straight at me, though I think his target was really Jennifer. The force of his attack left the pick embedded in the wood of the door frame, and I shouldered him aside and followed Jennifer through the door.

"Run!" I screamed at her, and grabbed her hand as I passed her. We hit the street and ran towards Studewood, where there would be businesses and the most traffic. And witnesses. I managed to work my phone out of my pocket as we ran, but I couldn't focus on it enough to call 911.

We were only a block from the busy street when we stumbled and Jennifer's hand was wrenched out of mine. I turned to see her on her ass on the pavement, the ice pick sticking out of her shoulder as she turned to kick and claw at her attacker.

Josh Katz stood over her, chest heaving and face red. Sweat was dripping from him – he was in no shape to be chasing people down the street. We probably would have outrun him if he hadn't been fueled by adrenalin and rage.

"You bitch!" Katz was screaming as he pawed at Jennifer, trying to get at the pick in her back.

I ran at him, trying to tackle him back off of Jennifer, but he was heavier and meaner and just brushed me aside. I fell and rolled a couple of times before I jumped back up and came at him from behind, trying to pull him away.

"The police!" I was shouting, hoping someone would hear. "Someone call the police!"

Katz started fighting me at that point, taking his hands off Jennifer and turning to push at me again, and I could feel his weight behind the attack. I flew back several feet, landing against a parked car before everything went black.

❧

"...rand? Mr. Hillebrand? Can you hear me?" a voice was saying. I didn't feel like answering, but I grunted.

"Mr. Hillebrand?"

I cracked one eye open and saw a blur that I thought might be Detective Perez looking at me. That didn't make sense, though, because the blur looked concerned. I blinked hard and tried opening my eyes again.

"Detective Perez?" I mumbled. Then, because I'm lame like that, I said the first thing that popped into my head. "You sure do have pretty hair."

She scowled then, and the world tilted back onto its axis. "He's awake," she said as she stood.

I tried looking around, but my head hurt and someone was shining a light in my eye. "Ow!" I batted at the light and it moved away.

"Looks like we've got a feisty one, Doug!" I heard a deep voice say.

"That's good. If they're feisty they'll be okay."

"Jennifer? Is Jennifer okay?" I tried to get up.

"Hold on there, tiger. Hold on. We've got to check you out."

I tried to sit still, but they sure seemed to be taking a long time. I could hear voices and sirens and see flashing red and blue lights out of the corner of my eye, but the two EMTs were blocking most of my field of vision.

"Please. Can you please just tell me if Jennifer is okay?" I asked again.

"She's feisty, too," said the first EMT, not-Doug.

I leaned my head back against the car where I was still sitting and let them finish doing what they needed to do.

"Can he talk yet?" I heard Petreski's voice from somewhere behind Doug. I was afraid to see him, afraid he would be angry, afraid this might be the last time.

"Yeah, he can talk. We should take him to the hospital for observation, though. He hit his head – he wasn't out for long, but he did lose consciousness."

"I'm fine. No hospital. I want to see Jennifer."

"I'll see what I can do," Petreski told the EMTs. They stepped aside and Petreski crouched down in front of me. He didn't look angry, but I didn't know how good an actor he was.

"Jennifer?" I asked, because I had to know. The last time I'd seen her she had an ice pick sticking out of her back and Katz had her on the ground.

"She'll be fine. She's on her way to the hospital, like you should be."

"What about Katz? It was Katz. He got into the house. He chased us down the street with a freaking ice pick."

Petreski shifted to one side, and beyond him I saw the bulk of Josh Katz, lying face down in the street. People in uniforms and jumpsuits were shuffling around him, but no one seemed overly worried about him.

"Oh my God. Is he dead? Did you have to shoot him to get him off of her?"

"No, nothing like that. He was like that when we got here. A witness said it looked like he had a heart attack or a stroke."

"He was pretty red in the face, and he was in bad shape. I'm surprised he was able to catch up to us." I closed my eyes so I wouldn't have to look at Katz anymore. "Can I go home now?" I asked.

"Soon. But first, would you please go to the hospital and get checked out? That way I can finish up here and I'll know you're safe. If you go, you can see Jennifer."

I opened my eyes to look at him. He smiled, just a small smile, but I knew we'd be okay. "Fine. But you have to come get me as soon as you're done here."

"I promise."

If You Feed Them, They Won't Leave

I DON'T know how long it takes to clear up a crime scene, but I remembered when we found Clarence it had seemed to go on forever.

I was in a curtained cubicle near the emergency room, and after they checked me over they seemed to forget about me, except for the young nurse who stuck her head in every once in a while to make sure I hadn't expired.

My phone was busted – I must have dropped it in my tussle with Katz – so I couldn't call anyone. All my numbers were in my phone, so I couldn't look anything up. I was pretty much stuck until Petreski came for me.

I was just starting to get irritable when he finally showed up, pulling back the curtain and looking me over. "They give you the all clear?"

"I don't know."

"Did you see Jennifer?"

"No. I think they've forgotten about me."

He went around the corner. I leaned my head back and closed my eyes. If anything needed to be done, Petreski – Ruben – would take care of it

"You ready to go?"

"Hmm?" I opened my eyes to see Petreski standing over me.

"You wanna go home?"

"God, yes," I said, sitting up and swinging my legs over the side of the bed. "They're letting me go?"

"I told them you were dangerous."

"Har har har."

He helped me to his car – I was sore and stiff from lying in bed all day. I think that was actually worse than getting slammed into a car. I was surprised at how tired I was, and I was starving.

"My phone is busted," I grumbled at the dashboard.

"We'll get you a new one."

"But I want to order a pizza and I don't have a phone."

"I'll take care of it when I get you home. A hot shower will do wonders for your aches and pains."

"Speaking from experience?"

"Yep."

I didn't like thinking about him getting tossed around and landing on cars so I didn't ask him any more questions.

We got to my building and he helped me up the stairs to my apartment. Don came out to the landing – we weren't exactly quiet and I can complain loudly when I want to.

"Oh my God! What happened to you?!"

"Josh Katz threw me at a car."

"What?!"

"He's fine," Petreski told him. "You can get the whole story tomorrow, okay?"

"Yeah, okay." Don stepped back into his apartment, scooping up Bridger who had come to investigate the commotion.

Petreski unlocked my door and I shuffled inside.

"Go take a shower," Petreski said, pushing me towards the bathroom. I nodded and moved in that direction.

"Don't peek!" I managed to call out as I headed in that direction.

"I'll, uh, do my best," Petreski said after a few seconds.

He was right about the shower, and by the time I emerged, dressed in clean clothes, my mental fog had lifted and a hot pizza was waiting for me.

"Beer?" Petreski asked. "The doctor said you don't have a concussion so it should be okay."

"Yeah."

He came back from the kitchen with two open beers and sat them on the coffee table before sitting next to me on the sofa.

"You haven't asked me about Katz."

"What about him? He came at us with an ice pick, so I'm assuming that was the murder weapon and he killed Wilton and Thrasher."

"Forensics is running tests, but I'm going to say that's likely the case."

"I knew it wasn't Helena Wilton."

"You didn't know. You had a theory." He picked up his beer.

"Yeah, but it was a really good theory, wasn't it?"

"I can't argue with that."

"The thing I'm wondering about, though, is the ice pick."

"What about it?"

"Why no one noticed it was missing, or no one identified an ice pick as the murder weapon."

"An ice pick was on the short list. And we did find a couple of ice picks at the Wilton house – they entertained quite a bit and had more than one fully stocked bar. But no one could say if all the ice picks there were accounted for. They're cheap and easily replaceable – not the kind of thing you inventory or keep track of or even think about."

"Unless you're looking for one and can't find it."

"Exactly. Is that what happened?"

"Yeah. Jennifer Katz was going to fix us a couple of drinks. The ice in the freezer was stuck together, but when she looked for the ice pick she couldn't find it. I was going to help her look for it, but when she described what it looked like… I just knew. I heard a noise from the service porch, so I tried to get us both out of there as quick as I could."

"That probably saved both your lives."

I shrugged. I didn't want to think about what could have happened.

He took a long swallow from his beer and returned it to the table.

"What?" I asked. I knew there was something.

"I need to tell you something… weird."

"And that would be different from anything else that's happened lately how?"

"Touché. But seriously, this is something you should know. About me."

"Shit, Ruben. You're starting to freak me out here."

"Yeah – that. See, I've never really liked the name Ruben."

"Oh, good. No offense, but it makes you sound like a sandwich, and it's kind of hard to say."

"I like it better when you call me Boo."

I blinked at him a couple of times before answering. "When… when have I called you Boo?" Although, I had a feeling I knew.

"It's kind of like how you just knew Raymond's name was Raymond."

I nodded, not taking my eyes off his face.

"When I was a kid, my little sister couldn't say Ruben. The closest she could get was Boo, and it stuck. My whole family calls me Boo now."

I kept sitting there, looking at him, at that steady green stare and his silky dark hair and I started getting pissed off.

"I think I need to drink my beer now," I said.

"Okay."

I drank about half of the beer, sitting there looking at him and processing this strange conversation.

"Jake? Are you… are you okay?"

"I'm not sure yet."

"Okay."

"I think I need to eat something. This is kind of big to process on an empty stomach."

He opened the pizza box and I saw that he had ordered my favorite again, but this time there were anchovies on his half. Of course there were.

"You can put anchovies on the whole thing next time," I said, and I could feel him relax next to me.

We devoured the pizza in silence. Where does a conversation go after something like that, anyway? I had questions – lots and lots of questions, but there was one thing that bothered me and needed to be addressed.

I put my plate down, wiped my hands on a paper towel, and turned to look him in the eye.

"I'm not entirely happy with you at the moment."

"I know. I'm sorry. .I would have –"

"Did you come around to spy on us? On me and Don? To find out if we knew anything?"

"No! I swear."

"So?"

"The first time I came it was that day you told me about Katz. At the coffee shop. I had seen you at the crime scene, but everything was moving so fast that morning… Anyway, when I saw you again, at Ground Up, it was like a gut punch, okay? I couldn't come as myself, so I came as Boo. I had to see you. You know why I kept coming back. Don't say you don't."

"But – but – I told Boo – told you! I told you all kinds of really personal, private stuff!"

Petreski settled back into the sofa and pulled me down with him. "I know! It was awesome!"

"It was not awesome! It was personal! I feel so… so exposed!"

"You didn't tell me anything embarrassing. It is nice to know that you think I'm hunky, though. Do you really think I'm hunky?"

"Not anymore I don't."

He buried his face in my neck and laughed. "You do! You *so* do!"

"Oh my gosh! You peeked! When I was in the shower! When I was getting dressed! You are such a pervert!"

He was still laughing when he answered. "Like you wouldn't have done the same thing in my place?"

I didn't answer, but I didn't push him away either. I probably should have been more shocked that Petreski was Boo, or Boo was Petreski, or whatever. But honestly? After everything else that had happened, it hardly seemed worth the energy.

"Perez is like you, isn't she?"

"Like me?"

"A… a… cat person? Werecat? Oh gosh, she is! That time Boo – you – brought the lady cat that didn't like me! Animals always like me. That was Perez, wasn't it?"

He nodded, like he didn't want to admit it. I thought about Perez, trying to remember something she had said that seemed strange at the time.

"Do you – I mean, werecats or whatever in general – do you have regular cats, as pets?"

"We just call ourselves Cat. And no, we like cats, but it would seem strange to us to keep one as a pet."

"Perez said something strange. We saw her at the pet store looking at cat treats. Don asked her if she had a cat and she said not at the moment. But it sounded funny when she said it. What did she mean?"

"That is really not my story to tell."

"She won't tell me, though, will she? She can barely be civil to me. If I can understand her better maybe I can figure out how to relate to her."

He sighed and leaned back. "She had a daughter."

"Had?"

"Yeah. Perez was just a rookie then. She was young and crazy in love. She got pregnant, and the guy took off. She kept the baby, named her Roxie. She was beautiful, and a little badass, just like her mom."

"What… what happened?"

"Leukemia. She just got sick one day, and kept getting sicker. It happened fast, and Perez has been angry ever since."

"But, the cat treats?"

"Roxie's father was human, but Roxie was Cat. Perez always called her Little Kitten. Towards the end, when Roxie had no appetite, cat treats were the only thing that she would eat, human or Cat."

"That is so freaking sad." I could feel myself starting to tear up. I wasn't sure I was ready to shed tears for Perez, but I could shed them for little Roxie.

"Yeah. Sometimes, when she's got it bad, she'll get the treats."

I wiped at my eyes with the back of my hand. "Okay. I need you to stop talking now."

He pulled me down next to him and I turned to lean into his strength. "Don't you dare tell Perez I cried."

"I wouldn't dare tell Perez that I told you about her daughter. She'll probably figure out that I did, but as long as I don't admit it she won't claw me up."

We stayed like that for a while, but me being me I had more questions.

"Do you – y'all – is there… do you… hmm. Is there such a thing as werewolves?"

"I don't know."

"How can you not know?"

"As far as I know I've never met one. I can't say for sure. I just know about Cats. That's enough to keep me busy. That, and murders, and you."

"Speaking of me…"

"Yes?"

"In the books there's this thing about mates. Is that real?"

"Only in books. You really need to start reading something other than paranormal romance. There's no mystical bond or anything like that. We're not bound. You can reject me, and it'll be like any other rejection. I'm not going to die or anything ridiculous like that."

"Oh, good." I was maybe a little disappointed. I sat up straight, so I could see his face. "But then, why? I mean, you moved in pretty fast, there, Detective Boo."

"Well, there's no mystical bond, but there's instinct. Scents and pheromones, that kind of thing. They're powerful for Cats, and those did draw me to you."

"So, basically, you like the way I smell."

"Something like that. Too weird?"

"Not any weirder than anything else that's happened lately."

"So, you're not going to kick me out?" He looked up at me, his green eyes hopeful and teasing.

"No, Boo, I'm not kicking you out. Besides," I leaned down to whisper in his ear, "I fed you. You have to stay."

Coming Soon

NOT A MERMAID

It's July in Houston, and heat waves and storm warnings have everyone on edge. When the rains finally come, Jake Hillebrand's strange dreams take a sinister turn, leading him to the body of a young woman in a flooded bayou. What appears at first to be a drowning turns out to be foul play, and Detectives Victoria Perez and Ruben "Boo" Petreski are on the case.

Jake tries to stay out of their way, but the problem with being friendly and approachable is that people keep wanting to tell him things he probably shouldn't know.

About the Location

Jake's neighborhood is a fictionalized version of my own "hometown" of Woodland Heights. Most of the locations are real, but portrayed fictionally. Some are based on real places, but the names are changed. If you were to ask me about any location in the book, I could take you to the spot(s) that inspired it. Jake and Don's apartment building is based on an apartment building I lived in myself. It is still standing, although others like it have sadly been lost in recent years. I love my neighborhood, and I grieve to see the so-called progress that is being inflicted upon it. If you feel that you need a 4,000 sf, 5 bedroom home with a 2-car garage, don't try to shoehorn it into a 5,000 sf semi-urban lot.

About the Author

Madeline Kirby lives in a Craftsman bungalow in Houston, Texas, with her husband, two cats, and a squirrelly neighbor who leaves pecan shells all over the front porch. If she's not at home writing, you'll probably find her at her local coffee shop.

You can follow Madeline on Twitter – @Madeline_Kirby – or check out her neglected blog, www.evilgeniusatwork.com.

Other Books by Madeline Kirby

Saving Grapes (Cable's Bend – Book 1)

Just That Easy

36415826R00130

Made in the USA
Middletown, DE
13 February 2019